THE
PHANTOM LIMB

William Sleator
AND
Ann Monticone

AMULET BOOKS
NEW YORK

Library of Congress Cataloging-in-Publication Data

Sleator, William.
The phantom limb / William Sleator, Ann Monticone.
p. cm.
Summary: Living in a dreary new home with his father dead, his mother hospitalized, and his grandfather increasingly distant, fourteen-year-old Isaac's wish for someone to reach out to him comes true in the form of a phantom arm that appears in a mirror box designed to help amputees, warning of danger.
ISBN 978-0-8109-8428-8
[1. Supernatural—Fiction. 2. Moving, Household—Fiction.
3. Grandfathers—Fiction. 4. Optical illusions—Fiction.
5. Loneliness—Fiction. 6. Mystery and detective stories.] I. Title.
PZ7.S6313Ph 2011
[Fic]—dc22
2011010396

THE ART OF BOOKS SINCE 1949

115 West 18th Street
New York, NY 10011
www.abramsbooks.com

1

FINALLY, FRIDAY AFTERNOON AND THE LAST bell—the moment he lived for. He bolted out of school. Another long week of hell over.

He didn't know, of course, that he was going to find the mirror box that day.

As usual, the Fitzpatrick twins were lurking in the playground. Hadn't they humiliated him enough by shoving him into his locker yesterday, for everyone at his new school to see? At school there was no way to avoid them. They were black-haired, identical, and hateful, and they wore matching outfits every day. Today it was a trendy Japanese T-shirt over their jeans. "You scream just like a little girl," one of them said, referring to the locker incident.

He didn't know whether it was DCynthia or Destiny. They were equally vicious.

"What's that sack you're wearing, shrimp?"

"It looks like it belongs to your father," the other said.

"Don't say anything about my father!" Isaac shot back, glaring at them. He was sorry the moment the words slipped out of his mouth, and he hurried to get away.

But there was something about the Fitzpatrick twins' taunts that rang true. He really was petrified about being in small spaces, like his locker. And now the whole school knew.

Nothing was going right in his life.

Why did his father have to die last year? Why did his mother have to start having seizures? Why did they have to move to the city? And now his weird grandfather was living with them, shuffling around the apartment in a daze and always getting in Isaac's way.

He was also lousy at sports, unlike Matt Kravetz, captain of the football team. If he were Matt Kravetz, the Fitzpatrick twins would be worshipping him, instead of taunting him relentlessly. He would be cool. Why did he have to feel like such a freak?

A mental darkness surrounded Isaac. He was fourteen, and he had no friends. He felt angry and miserable most of the time. He hated where he lived, who he lived with, and, most of all, himself.

But now it was Friday, and school was over, and he would be away from all of them. He looked forward to being alone, and for a while he could do whatever he wanted. He could read about his favorite subject—zombies—and imagine burying the Fitzpatrick twins alive or performing a ritual to make his grandfather go away. He could look at his collection of optical illusions and search for more on Google. He would have two and a half days of relief from the kids at school. Or one and a half days, anyway. With Monday looming so ominously, the empty feeling in the pit of his stomach would begin on Sunday. Friday was the best.

His mother, Vera, was a piano teacher. She had studied the piano at Juilliard and had met Isaac's father, Stan Verdi, at a reception after one of her performances. When his father was alive, they had lived in a nice house. His parents had dinner parties with interesting people—artists like his mother, scientists like his father. Isaac wasn't much for socializing, but he liked the background noise of their conversations and games.

But after his father had died unexpectedly in a plane crash in Africa, it turned out they couldn't keep the house. Vera couldn't handle the stress, and that's when she began having seizures. They had to move to a small apartment in the city. Sometimes Isaac felt as though he was suffocating in those tiny rooms. It was harder for him to be alone and lose himself in his collection of optical illusions. It was even harder living with his grandfather, who hadn't acted like himself in years. His behavior bothered Isaac so much that eventually they had had a major blowup. Now his grandfather was cowed and distant—but still in the way.

Vera's seizures had worsened. She couldn't teach anymore and was ordered to stay home. Then a special unit in a hospital about a hundred miles away was highly recommended as the best place for treating her symptoms, so they had to move again.

The hospital helped them find inexpensive housing, so they moved just before school started.

Even though the new place had two floors, the rooms were small and gloomy. It was a real contrast to the house they had lived in before his father died. But it did have a storage room where Isaac could display his optical illusions. Isaac often escaped to that room, where he could study his collection in peace.

When he got to the house, he locked his bike in the garage and went straight to the storage room upstairs.

There was still some stuff in the room that had belonged to the previous owners. The day Isaac saw the place for the first time, he had looked through their things quickly, once, and found some faded black-and-white pictures of an old man and woman with a boy and a girl. The real estate agent told them that the boy had died in the hospital, but he didn't know of what.

The boy had been looking straight into the lens when the picture was taken. When Isaac looked at the picture, it was as if the boy was looking at him.

He quickly refocused on his optical illusions. In the corner of the room was a table with an odd array of objects arranged on it. Isaac's collection.

He studied "The Snake," a jagged purple and green picture. When you looked at it from the side, it appeared to be moving menacingly toward you, even though it was really completely stationary. Next to it was "All Is Vanity," the famous picture of a beautiful woman looking in a mirror. But when you looked at it for a moment longer, the whole thing turned into a skull. He loved his real model of the Necker cube, which was an outline of a cube made out of wire whose front and rear surfaces kept seeming to switch back and forth, so that sometimes the cube appeared to be pointing right and other times left. Before Grandpa had gotten confused, he told Isaac that when the cube did that, it was rotating through the fourth dimension.

He was most proud of his actual model of the Menger sponge. He had seen drawings of this bizarre object in books about chaos and also online, and when he found out that someone had actually made a three-dimensional model of it, he had insisted on special-ordering it immediately. It was so delicate, it had to be hand-delivered to their door, cushioned and protected in many layers of padding.

It was a cube, about a foot on each side. A cube-shaped hole was cut out of each face of the cube.

Inside the empty cubes, a square hole was cut out of each surface. If you did this an infinite number of times, you ended up with an object that had infinite surface area and zero volume. If somehow you were actually *inside* something like this, everywhere you went you would be entering a smaller space than the one you had just left. That's what was so terrifying but also so intriguing about it. To Isaac, it had the fascination of a horror movie.

Grandpa had once explained how the cube worked. "An iteration is every time you make the next set of smaller holes. Theoretically, by the fiftieth iteration the cubicles are the size of atoms." Grandpa said that Isaac's model had only three iterations, or otherwise it wouldn't hold together at all. "A Menger sponge with four iterations made out of business cards would weigh a ton," he said.

Isaac really missed the old Grandpa and the way things used to be.

When he finally managed to drag his eyes away from the Menger sponge, there was a sudden bright glint. He blinked. Then he looked over by the window to see where the sparkle of light was coming from. But it wasn't coming from outside. Over in the pile of stuff the previous tenants had left, he saw an object he hadn't noticed before. It was unlike anything he had ever seen.

Isaac squatted down to examine the object. It was an open rectangular wooden box, simple and unadorned, with a bottom and four sides but no top. In one of the long sides there were two round holes that were just the right size so that you could stick your hands and forearms into the box. Inside the box—between the two holes and bisecting the box across its width—was a dusty mirror, with a reflecting surface on each side. That's what had caught his attention.

Isaac was fascinated. At first, he hesitated. Then, with his left hand on the floor, he stuck his right hand and forearm into the hole on the right side of the box. When he looked down into the box, he could see his right hand and arm, and also the reflection of his right hand and arm in the mirror. So it looked as if both his hands were inside the box. But he could *feel* his left hand on the floor. It was an extremely peculiar sensation to *see* his left hand in one place and at the same time *feel* it in another place. It was as if he had two left hands. He pulled his hand quickly out of the box, and the sensation stopped instantly.

It was an optical illusion all right! It sure felt weird

to see his hand in one place and feel it in another. Isaac had the very strong sensation that the box also had a real function. But what? Had it belonged to the boy in the picture—the boy who seemed to be staring at him? Had the dead boy put his hands into the box a lot? The thought gave Isaac the creeps.

Did the box have anything to do with the boy's death?

2

ISAAC REALLY WANTED TO TELL GRANDPA about this box with a mirror, but how could he? Grandpa lived in his own world. Mostly he stayed in his room. At first, Isaac had felt sorry for him, especially right after Gram died. Before she died, he had been so full of life—a brilliant physiologist who had done important research on the heart muscle. Isaac's interest in illusions and puzzles was because of Grandpa, who had helped him start his collection. But slowly Grandpa had slipped into another world. He could no longer do anything by himself. He had become a slob. At first, Isaac was just bored and annoyed with him. But after his father died and

Grandpa moved in with them, his presence became so unbearable that Isaac tried to avoid him as much as possible. His disdain pushed Grandpa further into his other world.

Isaac took the box to his room, dusted it off, and carefully put it on his bed. Then he went to the computer and logged on to Google. He typed in "box with a mirror" and read down the list of selections until he came to the one that said "mirror box." He clicked on it.

There were two pictures. Near the top was a man looking to his right, with two hands in front of him, each hand a different shade of gray. Near the bottom was a drawing of a mirror box, exactly like the one Isaac had just found. The text explained that a doctor named V. S. Ramachandran had invented the mirror box as a way of helping people who had had a limb amputated.

Obviously, some past tenant was an amputee. Then Isaac felt a chill. Had the teenage boy who died in the hospital been the amputee?

Isaac continued reading. The article reported that a very large percentage of amputees have what is called "phantom limb pain," which means that they feel pain—often excruciating pain—in the limb that has been cut off. Frequently, it feels as if the limb is bent into an uncomfortable position. Often, when an arm has been amputated, for example, the amputee feels that the missing hand is clenched—that the fingers and fingernails are pressing into the palm much harder than could ever happen with a real hand—and the pain of it is unbearable. Medications didn't help. Hypnosis didn't help. People had to live for years and years with this phantom pain— phantom, because the limb wasn't there. But the pain itself was very real.

Then this neurologist, Dr. Ramachandran, had the idea of making a mirror box. Let's say the person had a complete right arm and hand but his left arm had been amputated below the elbow. If he put his whole right arm into the right hole of the mirror box and then put his left arm, with the stump, into the left hole, and if he then looked down into the right side of the mirror, the reflection would show a complete arm and hand. Because a mirror image is reversed, the mirror showed *a left arm and hand.* It looked as if the amputated limb had somehow grown back. The amputee could move his complete arm and hand, and it would look as though his missing arm and hand were doing the same movements. So if he felt that his left hand was painfully clenched, he could *un*clench it by unclenching his right hand.

And when he did that, the pain went away.

It seemed unreal, like magic. But with patient after patient, the mirror box made the pain disappear. It was the only thing that worked.

Isaac was enthralled. Here was an optical illusion that wasn't just a game. It had a real function—as he had suspected—and it really helped people. He felt a macabre excitement.

Isaac clicked on more of the "mirror box" sites. He found an article that talked about bizarre sensations that two people could create with the mirror box. He spent so much time reading about the mirror box that, before he knew it, it was time for dinner—at least for Grandpa, who liked to eat early. Resentfully, Isaac left the box and went down to the kitchen.

Their old house had had a large dining room. The dinner parties there had been full of stimulating conversation and laughter, which Isaac used to hear from his room. His father was always telling humorous and fascinating stories about his travels, entertaining everybody. He had been a primatologist, and every summer the three of them had gone to

Africa and lived in the jungle so his father could study chimpanzees. Isaac wished his father were here now so he could share the mirror box with him.

His mother had often played the piano at their parties, and the guests had listened intently. The food she cooked was always wonderful.

Before checking into the hospital, Vera had cooked and frozen some of her best meals, so that there would be food available that Isaac could prepare quickly and easily for him and his grandfather. He pushed things around in the freezer until he found the chili, his favorite. He needed comfort food tonight, after the bad week at school and his fascination with—and confusion about—the mirror box.

He thawed the chili in the microwave and found the generic sauce for it in the fridge. He got it all ready and then went upstairs and knocked on Grandpa's door. He heard Grandpa get up. Isaac waited for him and then followed as he shuffled downstairs.

There was no dining room in this house. They ate their meals in the little breakfast alcove off the kitchen, called a nook, which had a built-in plastic table like a cheap diner and a small window in the corner. Isaac and Grandpa sat across from each other. Grandpa stared out the window, but it was clear from his blank expression that he wasn't really seeing anything. As usual, he hadn't shaved or combed his hair.

Isaac brought Vera's steaming chili out on warmed-up plates. Her chili *was* amazing. It didn't have ground beef; instead, the meat was in soft cubes, like a stew. There was a lot of garlic in it. Isaac missed the special sauce Vera used to put on it—*pico de gallo,* which had lots of real chili peppers, red onions, tomatoes, lime juice, cilantro, and fresh avocados. It was wonderfully spicy, but not *too* spicy. Just exactly right for Isaac's taste. He could never find anything like it in a restaurant.

Isaac dug in with gusto. Grandpa, as always, just picked at his food. He never seemed to notice what he was eating; clearly, it didn't make any difference to him.

Isaac would have liked to tell the former Grandpa about the mirror box and what it was for and how well it worked. Instead, he kept his discovery to himself and thought back to the young boy who used to live here. He must have had an arm amputated. Isaac wondered why.

Another of the online articles had mentioned a game of sorts that two people can play with a mirror box. Isaac wished there was someone he could try it with, but there was no one around.

He was almost finished with his dinner when he heard a loud noise. He looked over at Grandpa and saw that he had spilled his bowl of chili all over his lap.

"Damn it, Grandpa! Now you've really made a mess!" Isaac said angrily, as though speaking to an errant child. He sighed. Dinner was ruined.

He took Grandpa up to his room to change and then headed back to the kitchen.

When he had finished cleaning up the mess, he brought the mirror box down to the living room and put it on the coffee table. Grandpa had come down again in his clean clothes and was sitting on the couch. Isaac, feeling guilty for the way he had yelled at him, knelt on the floor next to the box and placed it so that Grandpa could reach it from the couch. He thought about how he had put one hand in and kept the other one out and about how weird it had felt. But putting both hands in was supposed to be even weirder. He hadn't tried it yet.

Grandpa was watching him.

Now Isaac slowly put both of his forearms into the box. He looked at the right side of the mirror and moved his right hand back and forth but kept his left hand still. He felt a jolt of surprise and couldn't keep from laughing nervously. "This feels so strange!" he said. "To *see* my left hand move—and to *feel* it not moving."

Then Isaac had to leave the room briefly to go to the bathroom. When he came back, Grandpa was doing the same thing Isaac had done with the mirror box. Isaac's sense of guilt disappeared. He didn't want anybody else to touch the box, especially Grandpa. "Get away from that!" he ordered.

Grandpa quickly put his hands in his lap.

When Isaac calmed down, he talked to himself, as though Grandpa were invisible. "Now I can try it the other way around." Again he put both arms into the box. Looking into the right side of the mirror, he moved his left hand but not his right. He felt an even more powerful jolt. "This is even weirder," he said. "To feel my left hand move and see that it's not moving. It's like I have a third hand—an invisible hand."

Grandpa didn't say anything, but he kept watching.

"The article said it's because the brain hates contradictions," Isaac said. "It can't make sense of seeing its body in different places." He paused. "OK—

now this is supposed to be the weirdest of all." Isaac put his hands back into the box, once again looking into the right side of the mirror. He needed someone to help him, so he said, "Grandpa, could you take your finger and run it across my right hand?"

Acting as if they were playing Simon Says, Grandpa followed Isaac's instructions exactly. Isaac watched his left hand being touched, but the hand itself felt nothing. He shivered. "Jeez, it's like my left hand has no feeling in it at all—like it's a dead hand. This isn't just weird, it's creepy!"

Grandpa shook his head and left the room, but Isaac barely noticed. He was too preoccupied with his new find.

3

STOP THAT RACKET!"

In another house, at a different time, an eight-year-old girl was struggling at the piano.

"I said stop!" the voice screamed. "Your hands are banging like hams on that keyboard and you're giving me a headache. Make yourself useful and help me with dinner. Let your brother play."

The girl calmly went upstairs, got her doll, and locked herself in the bathroom. "I'll help you, baby," she said, holding her doll in front of the mirror. "We don't need anybody else." She pulled at the doll's arm.

4

THE NEXT DAY, SATURDAY, ISAAC WENT TO the hospital to visit Vera for the first time since she had been admitted. He hated the hospital, but he had run out of excuses not to go. It was close enough to their house that he could bike there easily.

The night his mother was admitted had been a nightmare. After she was settled in her room, he had made the mistake of taking the elevator instead of going down the stairs. He hated small spaces and usually avoided elevators, but he wanted to get out as fast as possible. He also hated how sterile and cold the hospital was, how washed out everything looked under the fluorescent lights. The hallways all looked the same. And even though many people were there, it was eerily quiet.

In his rush to leave, he pushed the wrong button, and he ended up in the basement without realizing it. When the doors opened and he stepped out, he found himself among a long series of connected cavelike corridors, shadowy and confusing. It was a dark, underground maze. He was confronted with signs that said things like MORGUE, ENDOSCOPY, RADIATION THERAPY, and ENVIRONMENTAL SERVICES, but there was no exit sign. He started to panic. He was sweating. He sat down for a few minutes, taking slow, deep breaths to regain his composure.

When he felt a little better, he got up and looked around again. At last he found a door that said EMERGENCY EXIT. He ignored the warning about an alarm going off and pushed his way out the door. He could hear the noise behind him as he ran to get a taxi in the blissful open space of outside.

Today when he got to the hospital, he made sure to walk up the stairs. When he reached the sixth floor, he reluctantly pushed through the door that said INTENSIVE CARE — LIMITED ACCESS.

The nurse who had been there when his mother was admitted was sitting behind a computer at the nurses' station. Her name tag said CANDI: CHARGE NURSE. She wore bright pink lipstick, and she greeted Isaac with a smile. He showed her his ID, which was required to get into the intensive care unit.

"How are you today?" she asked him.

"I'm OK, I guess. How's my mother?"

Candi looked worried. "Well, she's pretty heavily sedated right now, I'm afraid. Dr. Ciano keeps . . ." She stopped herself. It was probably against hospital ethics for a nurse to criticize a doctor. "When she's not so sedated, though, she's a delight," Candi said. "She likes to talk about music."

"She's a pianist," Isaac said. "I forget what room she's in."

"Six thirty-eight," Candi said. "Be sure to wash your hands." She smiled.

Isaac was shocked. On his way to his mother's room he passed the Fitzpatrick twins wearing matching pink-and-white uniforms. What were they doing volunteering in a hospital anyway? Helping people wasn't their style. It seemed he was never going to escape them. Thankfully, they ignored him.

Vera was in a room with two beds, but one was empty. Her room was small, with one window looking out at a brick building just a few feet away. She was lying in the bed near the door. Her eyes were closed, and her right hand was attached to an IV—a needle that was connected to a tube that went to a bag of liquid hanging on a metal pole. The liquid, whatever it was, was slowly entering her bloodstream. It occurred to Isaac that she must hate being bound to the IV and not able to move around without help.

He went over to the sink and washed his hands.

A female doctor came in and repositioned his mother's arm. *There must be something wrong with the IV line,* Isaac thought. Now he was concerned about her. Vera's eyes fluttered open, and she winced. Isaac could see that the doctor was awkward.

"Sorry," the doctor said to Vera.

Vera looked down at her arm, then at Isaac. "Dr. Ciano, this is my son, Isaac."

The doctor had a mass of unruly dark hair. She turned toward Isaac with a forced half smile. Then she looked at her watch. "I've got rounds now," she said, and left the room quickly.

Vera had long black hair and was very good-looking, especially now that she wasn't wearing all the heavy makeup she usually had on. "Hey, Ize," she said sleepily. She smiled at him, then yawned. "It's so good to see you. How's it going?"

"OK, I guess. I found this really cool thing in that storage room in the house." He began telling her about the mirror box, but her eyes started to close again. "It's not important, though. How are you doing?" he asked her.

She opened her eyes. "It's hard to tell with this horrible IV. I don't know what they put in it, but it either keeps me asleep or puts me into a stupor so I hardly feel anything." She shrugged. "But the nurses have been so wonderful, especially Candi—not like that odd Dr. Ciano. She has the personality of a crow."

They both laughed. At that moment, Vera sounded like her old self. "She has no bedside manner," she went on, "and I'm not sure she knows what she's doing. She just has me in bed on an IV, drugged." She sighed. "But this is the hospital that everyone recommended." Her eyes fluttered shut again.

She had fallen asleep. Even though Isaac was worried about her, he was relieved to be able to leave the hospital and go back home.

As he was leaving, he asked Candi if there was a men's room nearby.

"Why don't you use the bathroom in your mother's room?" Candi said. "As long as you're scrupulously clean about it."

"No, that's OK," Isaac said, feeling embarrassed. "It's so small."

"A little claustrophobic?" Candi said. "Don't worry. Lots of perfectly normal people feel exactly the same way."

After going to the men's room near the ward, Isaac took the stairs to get out, continuing to avoid the elevator.

The next morning, Isaac woke up with his usual Sunday dread. He hated Sundays. Tomorrow was Monday. Tomorrow was school. Tomorrow the ridicule would start all over again.

He spent most of the day doing homework. He really did like some of it, especially the book they were studying in honors English class, *The Time Machine*. But he found it hard to concentrate, because all he could think about was how out of place he felt at school. As the day went on, he got more and more depressed.

He remembered the first time the Fitzpatrick twins had spotted him as the new kid. "Where'd you come from, Munchkinland?" they asked him. They nudged the girl they were with and all three of them laughed. "If the wind was any stronger, it would blow him away." They all laughed again. Isaac didn't know what to do except turn and walk away in shame.

Isaac needed to get his mind off school, so he went to get the mirror box, hoping it would distract him. There was something that attracted him to it intensely, more than any of his other optical illusions. It was a little scary to be so obsessed with something a dead amputee boy may have used. He kept thinking about the way the boy seemed to be staring at him from his picture.

But it was still only the beginning.

5

ISAAC GOT UNDRESSED AND CLIMBED INTO BED. But he couldn't sleep. The mirror box was on his desk, next to his computer. He got up, turned on the overhead light, sat down at his desk, and slid both his hands into the mirror box. While he looked in the mirror, he clenched and unclenched his right hand.

This time, the reflection of his hand in the mirror didn't move.

He cried aloud and jerked out his hands as fast as lightning.

The hand in the mirror remained where it was.

Now Isaac was terrified. "What *is* this?" he shouted, forgetting about not waking up Grandpa. It was impossible! How could there still be a hand in there when he had already removed his? He must be dreaming it.

Something made him slide his arms back into the box; they felt prickly, as if they'd fallen asleep. He let them rest on the bottom of the box without moving.

Suddenly, the hand in the mirror waved at him, as if in greeting.

He cried out again, but this time he left his hands in the box, watching for the hand in the mirror to make its next move. The moves did not match Isaac's hand. More and more it began to seem—even while being impossible—that the hand in the mirror was not a reflection.

Isaac couldn't fall asleep that night. He was too excited about the mirror box. He sat up in bed, leaned close to his desk, and peered back into the right side of the mirror. The impossible hand wasn't there.

Maybe he *had* imagined the whole thing. He hoped his mind was just playing tricks on him.

Did he dare put his hands inside it again and see what happened? He got out of bed and paced around the room, trying to decide what to do, walking softly so as not to wake Grandpa.

He was scared. But he was also very curious. He approached the mirror box slowly. His entire emotional reaction to it had changed. Before, it had almost glowed with fascination. Now its appearance was morbid, sinister. He put his fingertips into the holes, closed his eyes, and moved his hands into the box. He stood there for a long moment with his eyes squeezed shut, afraid to open them. But he couldn't resist. He opened them and looked at the right mirror.

He wasn't prepared for what he saw. He managed not to scream, but just barely. The hand in the mirror was holding something. Isaac focused his eyes to study what the hand held.

It was a smiley face button.

He had had one like it when he was younger, but this one was different. This one was woven. And this smile wasn't happy. No, it was cynical. Mocking. Isaac couldn't believe it. Was he going crazy? Was he hallucinating? He couldn't stand it a second longer. He pulled out his hands.

The hand in the mirror box waved the cloth face at him and pulled out too.

Isaac sank down onto his bed feeling exhausted. But he was too nervous—too scared—to sleep. What was going on here? How could the mirror box be doing this insane thing? Showing him a creepy, weird smiley face. Who was behind it? How could they be doing it? And why?

And that was when the thought first occurred to him: Maybe the phantom limb in the mirror box was trying to tell him something.

6

ISAAC WAS STILL AWAKE WHEN HIS ALARM
clock went off. He was very drowsy, and it took
him a moment to get his bearings. Then it came back
to him: the mirror box.

During the night he had put the haunted box in
his closet so that the awful specter would be out of
sight. But he hadn't been able to stop thinking about
it. As a result, he hadn't gotten any sleep at all.

He toyed with the idea of skipping school. After
all, he could use the excuse that his mother was in
the hospital.

It was seven A.M. Isaac dressed and went downstairs. Unbelievably, Grandpa was already in the

kitchen, sitting at the table. His hair was still unkempt, but at least his shirt was buttoned the right way.

Isaac sighed as he fried a couple of eggs and then put them on plates for the two of them. It was hard enough dealing with his own problems; being responsible for Grandpa was an added burden.

"How . . . is she doing?" Grandpa asked suddenly, startling Isaac.

So Grandpa wasn't lost in his own world, as he usually was.

"Well, it's hard to tell how she—" Isaac's cell phone rang, interrupting the conversation. Who could be calling?

"Hi, Ize," said his mother, sounding a little hoarse.

"Mom?" He hadn't expected that she would be alert enough to call him.

"I'm not as sedated today," Vera said. "Can you bring me some stuff before you go to school?"

His heart sank. Go back to the awful hospital again? But Vera was coherent; how could he refuse?

She wanted any bills that had collected and also her checkbook, the piano technique book she was reading, her music magazines, some cosmetics, and her glasses. It would all fit in his bicycle basket. Isaac sighed and said, "OK."

When he reached the hospital, he again walked up the six flights of stairs.

When he got to Vera's floor, he was relieved to see a friendly face. Candi greeted him pleasantly at the nurses' station. "No school today?" she asked.

"Mom called and said she needed some stuff from home. She doesn't seem so out of it today. I figured I could help her and then go to school a little late."

"Yes, fortunately Dr. Ciano decided your mother didn't need to be so sedated anymore." Candi smiled, and her voice softened. "Is that a book about piano playing?" she asked, looking at the pile of things he held in his arms.

"Yeah," he said.

"Don't forget to—"

"I know. Wash my hands," Isaac interrupted her, and they both laughed.

Today Vera sat propped up in her narrow hospital bed, not dozing the way she was the last time. But now she had tubes in both of her hands. Dr. Ciano was there, standing on the other side of the bed. She was adjusting the new IV.

"Ize!" Vera said with a big smile. She was like a whole different person. "It's great to see you. Thanks so much for bringing my things."

"Wait a minute. I have to wash my hands." He put her stuff down on the bedside table.

Dr. Ciano looked up from the new IV line for a moment. "Oh, a book about piano playing," she said. "I studied piano for a little while, but I wasn't any good at it. My brother was, though." She sighed. "OK, all done." She left the room without another word, but with her forced half smile.

Isaac took off his jacket and sat in the chair next to the bed. "What's happening?" he asked, looking around the room.

"Oh, you know. Always lots of fun around here." Vera rolled her eyes. She wasn't as sedated, but she still seemed a little loopy. "What about your breakfast? Did you eat?" she asked him. "There's a café down in the lobby."

"I made eggs. And guess what? When I got up, Grandpa was down there waiting, and he actually asked about you."

"Really?" Vera said.

There was a knock on the door. It was Dr. Ciano again. She walked toward the bed.

"Oh. Hello again, Dr. Ciano," Vera said nervously.

Isaac noticed that the doctor didn't wash her hands when she came in, which he found strange. He stood up so she could sit in the chair next to the bed. But instead she remained standing, leafing through a sheaf of papers. "You may not remember," she said to Vera, "but when you were admitted, we did an EEG. The EEG had some abnormalities, so I'd like to do some more extensive tests, like an MRI—just in case."

"Abnormalities? What kind of abnormalities?" Isaac asked.

"They could be anything, really, but I'm sure it's nothing to worry about."

"Oh," Isaac said, glancing quickly at his mother.

Dr. Ciano looked at him. "What day is it? Shouldn't you be in school?"

"My mother asked me to bring her some stuff," Isaac said, snapping at the doctor.

"Isaac," Vera said, eyeing him. "Don't be rude."

Dr. Ciano turned her attention back to Vera. "I'll be keeping you on the IVs until we have a better sense of what's wrong. I have to go now, but ring for one of the nurses if you need anything."

"When will you be back?" Isaac asked.

"I may be going to an out-of-state conference soon, but don't worry—I'm always around," the doctor said, and left the room.

"She's kind of weird, isn't she?" Isaac said very

softly. "What does all that mean, anyway? EEG and MRI?"

"They're different tests that measure brain activity," Vera replied. "But you know, I can't figure out why this hospital came so highly recommended. Dr. Ciano is so *peculiar*. She makes me uneasy. I wonder what she's telling them to put into these IVs." She yawned. "I'm feeling tired again. I might just close my eyes for a second," she said, her voice shaky. She quickly drifted off to sleep.

Isaac stayed with her while she slept. As long as he was at the hospital he could use it as an excuse to skip school. Which was worse? The hospital or school? It was hard to choose.

Isaac reached into his backpack and pulled out his zombie book. It was a relief to concentrate on something else.

A couple of hours later, the door opened. Another patient was wheeled into the room. She had short gray hair and a look of authority about her, despite being a patient. Isaac hated that she was there. And the commotion woke Vera, who looked surprised at first. After a moment she pulled herself together and greeted her new roommate warmly.

"Hi, I'm Vera, and this is my son, Isaac."

"Esther Kaplan. Nice to meet you both."

Candi entered the room and attached the new patient's IV bag to the permanent pole. "I'm sure you two will get along very well," she said. "Vera's a pianist. And you?"

"I'm a doctor," Esther told her. Then she paused. "You look familiar. Have you worked at other hospitals?"

"A lot of people say that. I just have one of those faces," Candi said. "Now, if you'll excuse me, I've got to see to some other patients." She smiled at them all as she left the room.

"So you're a doctor?" Vera said.

"Well, used to be. Retired now," Esther said. "I'm sure I've seen that nurse somewhere . . ."

"Maybe here in the hospital," Vera suggested.

"No, I don't think so," Esther said. "Oh, I don't know."

Isaac was relieved to finally leave the hospital. While he was riding to school on his bike, all of his worries came to a head: school and the Fitzpatrick twins, his mother's illness, Grandpa and that box. The thoughts sat in his stomach like a lump of lead. He decided he couldn't face school, so he headed home.

At home, he thought about the mirror box. What would happen the next time he put his arms in? He was scared . . . but he was more curious than anything. He reasoned that since it was now the middle of the day—and not the middle of the night—he could experiment with it again. He suddenly felt wide awake and alert. Anything that happened now had to be real, not the result of fatigue or his imagination.

Isaac remembered the way the hand in the mirror had shown him the woven smiley face and then had waved at him. *Was* it mocking him, just like the twins? Or was it trying to tell him something?

His heart began to speed up as he ascended the stairs and went into his room. He was hoping more than anything that the hand in the mirror wasn't real. He had too many things to worry about already—he didn't need to add "menacing hand" to the list.

Isaac stood in front of his closet door. His hand moved to the doorknob, then pulled back. He turned and prepared to walk away. He wasn't ready to risk putting his hands inside that thing again. But something urged him on, some nagging need to figure out what was happening. He turned back and made himself open the door.

There was the box, right where he had left it . . . except that the side with the holes was facing to the right. Was that how he had put it in there? He thought that the holes had been facing toward the door. He wasn't sure. Tentatively, he reached into the closet and pulled out the box. He had to get this over with.

Nothing will happen, he kept reassuring himself.

He put the box on his desk, sat down in front of it, took a deep breath, and slid his hands inside. It was a cool day, but he could feel sweat forming on his forehead. At first, he felt relieved to see only the reflection of his own hand.

But then the image disappeared, and the phantom limb came into view. It was holding a tattered piece of fabric with a faded yellow smiley face on it. Half of the smile was unraveled.

Isaac squeezed his eyes shut. Forcing his muscles to obey him, he kept his hands, trembling, inside the box.

The phantom limb was real after all. He hadn't imagined it.

But what was the hand trying to tell him?

Whose hand was it?

Isaac had so many questions but lacked any answers.

The hand could only sign to him, not speak—so how could he understand what it was trying to tell him?

He slowly opened his eyes again. He was just in time to see what happened next.

With a sudden violent movement, the phantom limb yanked a thread, and the smile unraveled completely.

7

THE TEN-YEAR-OLD GIRL STOOD IN THE kitchen, peeling potatoes that her mother was going to cook for dinner. She was smiling as she listened to the music that was being played in another room.

The music was coming from her brother. He was twelve now, a brilliant pianist—a prodigy, everyone said.

She had tried to learn to play the piano, but she was just no good at it. After a while, her mother had refused to keep paying for her lessons.

The girl finished peeling the last potato and dropped it into the kettle full of cold water. She cleared her throat. "All done," she said softly because she didn't want to interrupt the music. Her mother, who had been standing in the doorway listening blissfully to the piano, turned and looked at her.

"Did you cut them up?" her mother asked. She came over and looked into the pot and saw that the potatoes were still whole. "Give me the knife, please, and go work on your homework until dinner is ready."

The girl handed her the knife and left the kitchen. She went as quietly as possible up the stairs. She didn't do her homework, though. Instead, she picked up her baby doll and locked herself in the bathroom.

8

I SAAC WAS STILL TREMBLING SLIGHTLY AS HE put the dreadful box back into the closet. He was consumed with a million thoughts. He couldn't understand why the phantom limb had unraveled the smiley face.

At lunch, he sat across from Grandpa. The sandwiches Isaac had made were good, but not as good as Vera's.

"Did you find out anything at the hospital?" Grandpa asked, snapping Isaac out of his momentary distraction.

Again, Isaac was so surprised at Grandpa's question

that he was tongue-tied for a moment. He and Vera had both assumed that Grandpa's dim state of mind was permanent and would only get worse. But now Grandpa was actually speaking, and making sense. How was this possible?

"They did some tests on her brain, and they came out abnormal. They're going to do more tests and really check her out," Isaac said. "But her doctor is real weird about the whole thing and has her on all these medications that make her groggy."

"Oh," Grandpa said. He turned away and stared vacantly out the window, as usual. "Maybe I'll drive us over there sometime."

Not on your life, Isaac thought. He wouldn't get in a car with Grandpa in a million years. The last time, Grandpa had fallen asleep at the wheel on a crowded highway and ended up veering toward another car. "Grandpa! Wake up!" Isaac had screamed. Grandpa woke up instantly and said, "I was only asleep for a little while."

Isaac rode his bicycle back over to the hospital late that afternoon in a light rain. He really didn't want to return, but he needed money. He figured his mother must have taken her purse with her—he had checked, and it wasn't at home. Her ATM card must be in it. She didn't need it in the hospital.

He didn't see Candi. But he heard two familiar, shrill voices—there, in doll-like matching white and pink–striped uniforms, were the Fitzpatrick twins.

"Loser," one sneered openly, now that Candi wasn't around. She added, very softly so the other nurses wouldn't hear, "I bet you're really worried about your mommy." She smiled. "Oh, and don't forget—the hospital has lockers too."

Isaac looked down. When he looked up, he caught the other twin's eye—the one who hadn't insulted him. Her eyes met his for a moment.

"DCynthia, Destiny—I need you," one of the nurses called.

They left without another word.

Isaac watched them as they walked away, and then he headed down the hall to his mother's room. As he entered the room, he saw that Dr. Ciano was standing over Vera. She looked surprised to see him. "I was just doing one last check before going off to my conference," she said, and left.

"Mom, sorry to bring this up, but I'm out of cash."

Esther was watching them from the other bed.

"Take my ATM card," Vera said. "It's in my purse, over there in the cabinet."

He stuck the card in his wallet and took a last look at her.

That was when he noticed it: a sore just below her right elbow, an odd bluish color. How had it gotten there?

He was shocked and really concerned.

9

EVEN THOUGH ISAAC WAS WORRIED ABOUT
his mother, he had something else on his
mind: the puzzling behavior of the phantom limb in
the mirror box. Maybe, he thought, if he found out
more about the people who had lived in his house
before them, he could solve the mystery of the mirror
box—where it had come from, what its purpose was.

But where should he begin? He knew that the
young boy had been sick and was a patient at the
hospital. Could he find his file? He doubted that any
hospital employee would give him that information—
these things were confidential.

As he left Vera's room, one of the twins appeared. "How's your mom doing?" she asked.

It was DCynthia—the one who had looked at him earlier, when Destiny was mocking him. He was surprised at her caring tone, but it was also confusing. Either she was setting him up for a joke or she was genuinely concerned. Was it possible that the twins weren't so mean when they weren't together?

"Not great, but thanks for asking," he said shyly.

Isaac wondered if he could ask DCynthia for help. Since she was only a volunteer and not a hospital employee, she might be willing to bend the rules if he asked her nicely. "Um . . . would you . . . do you think . . . could you maybe help me with something?" he forced himself to say.

She shrugged. "It depends," she said, looking over her shoulder to make sure her sister wasn't watching. "Why? What's up?"

"I need to get some information—about the people who lived in my house before us. Is there any way that you can look them up on the computer?"

DCynthia raised her left eyebrow. "Really?" she said slowly. "Well . . . I've watched the nurses use it. I know the password." Isaac knew that the twins liked being mischievous and breaking rules. She looked around. The nurses all seemed to be somewhere else. "Just keep an eye out for staff," she said as she hurried to the computer. Isaac heard her whisper the word "Orwell" under her breath. "What's your address?"

"77 North Union Street," Isaac said.

"Damn! The people who lived at this address before you were at County, not City, Hospital. But it still shows up on our network," DCynthia said. Luckily, she knew how to access the network.

She worked quickly, but it still took her a while. Finally, she grabbed a piece of paper, wrote something on it, and turned off the computer. She handed the paper to Isaac. "Here's their name, their new address, and their phone number."

Isaac looked at her. "Wow, thanks," he said. He carefully folded the paper and put it in his wallet.

"You're welcome," she said. "But this is between you and me."

Isaac was grateful that she hadn't asked him any questions. For the first time in a long time, he didn't feel angry.

Just then Destiny appeared. "What are you doing talking to this freak?" she said.

"I—I wasn't," DCynthia said. "He was talking to me about something stupid, just asking me why we volunteered here. I told him we had to. Community service for—you know. Forget it. He is seriously disturbed. Let's go."

As soon as he was outside, Isaac took out his phone and dialed the number. The name DCynthia had written down was "Haynes." After a few rings, a man answered. He sounded old, even older than Grandpa.

"Hi, uh . . . is this . . . um . . . Mr. Haynes?" Isaac asked.

"Yeah. Who's this?" the man answered gruffly.

"My name is Isaac. I know this is random, but I was wondering if you might be able to help me. I'm living in the house you used to be at—77 North Union Street. And . . . in the storage room I found this mirror box . . ."

"Yeah, so?" The man didn't sound at all interested.

"Well, I've been doing some research, and I know what the mirror box is for, and . . . Listen, could we talk in person? I was wondering about who it used to belong to and where it came from. You see, my mother, who's in City Hospital right now, is . . . um . . . having some problems there. Her doctor is strange and stuff, and if you could answer some of my questions, it might help me figure out . . ." Isaac trailed off. He couldn't gather his thoughts. He felt completely flustered.

"I don't know what you're talking about," the man said sternly.

"Please, if we could just meet for a minute, I could explain what I mean . . ."

"I don't have time for this," the man said, and hung up.

Embarrassed but undeterred, Isaac waited a few minutes and then called again. He was determined to get some answers.

This time a woman answered. "You want to know about Joey?" she asked, so softly that Isaac could barely hear her.

Isaac grabbed at the chance. "Yes!" he said. "Because whoever the mirror box belonged to, I'm curious about him."

"My husband is going out in half an hour," the woman whispered. "Come over then."

"But where?"

"I'll meet you in front of the building," she whispered.

Then the line went dead.

10

THE GIRL'S BROTHER WAS THIN AND SICKLY,
yet he was devoted to practicing the piano as
much as possible. He liked to compare himself to
Frédéric Chopin, the famous composer and pianist
who lived from 1810 to 1849. Chopin, who was also
thin and sickly, died young.

When her brother was sick, as he often was, the
girl took care of him.

She *liked* taking care of him. It made her feel
needed and important, qualities she never felt when
she was around kids her own age, or her teachers, or
her mother.

She knew that he looked forward to her visits to his

sickroom, when she'd bring him a tray with a bowl of chicken noodle soup or a cup of hot chocolate. Plus she always added special treats. Then, while he slowly ate or drank—he was never that hungry—she would tell him stories about school. Mostly they were made up. Her brother had already finished high school; he was waiting until he was well enough to attend the prestigious music conservatory that had given him a full scholarship.

Because they spent so much time together, they became very close. Now, whenever their mother got mad at her, her brother would defend her.

One day, while their mother was out, the girl explored her bureau and found her prescription pills. She experimented using them on her brother. He just got sicker and sicker. She kept giving him the pills.

Although his health rapidly deteriorated, he still managed to hobble down the stairs to the piano. But his playing was different now because he was so weak. He fumbled and made more mistakes than he had before.

Eventually, he couldn't even make it downstairs. All he could do was listen to music in bed, music he wished he was creating.

When her brother died, the doctors didn't understand why. They couldn't figure out what caused him to become so sick.

After her brother's death, she began reading medical books, studying whatever she could get her hands on.

She knew what she wanted to do.

She wanted to become a doctor.

11

AFTER HE HUNG UP, ISAAC HOPPED ON HIS bike and rode off to meet the woman he had just spoken to.

Now he had a name to associate with the mirror box: Joey. But why was the man unwilling to tell him anything? And why did the woman have to keep it a secret from her husband? Most important of all, how could he persuade the woman to tell him what he needed to know?

By the time he found the address, he was panting and sweaty from the bike ride. It turned out to be a brick apartment house. With its large glass double doors, it looked like some kind of institution. An old lady who was wearing a baggy brown dress and holding a cane was standing on the sidewalk. She almost seemed to be hiding behind a tree.

He hopped off his bike and walked over to her, wheeling the bike beside him. "Mrs. Haynes?" he said. "I'm Isaac."

"You're the boy who called?" she asked. "The boy with Joey's mirror box?"

"That's me. So it *was* Joey's box?"

"We can't talk here," she said, pulling at Isaac's arm. "If anybody sees me with you, they'll tell Harry. Come on. This way." She started off down the street, back in the direction Isaac had come from. There were storefronts along the block. "Here," she said, pointing to a parking lot behind a drugstore.

The old woman was breathing heavily by now and looked as if she needed to sit down. But of course there was no place to sit, so they just stood.

"When you called," she said, "what did you mean about your mother being in the hospital and having problems with the doctor? What does that have to do with my grandson Joey?"

Isaac realized that she must have been listening in on his conversation with the old man. She was clearly rushed, and she seemed so terrified of being seen that he didn't know how to explain everything. He figured he might as well get right to the point. "Was Joey ever in City Hospital? Did he have a doctor named Ciano?"

"Joey was in County Hospital, not City. And I forget the doctor's name."

"Oh," Isaac said, surprised and disappointed. Then he quickly continued. "I've been using the mirror box, just fooling around. And then I began to see that the hand in the mirror was different from my hand, doing different things."

The old woman's mouth dropped open. She put her hand to her chest and looked at him sharply. "Is this some kind of cruel joke?" she said, her voice rising.

"No, it's not a joke," Isaac said. "I know it sounds absurd, but it's true. I think he's been . . . well, trying to communicate with me."

"That's—that's not possible. How could he do that?"

"What if . . . what if he's trying to tell me something? Something about my mother? Listen," Isaac said, knowing how crazy he sounded. "Something weird is going on at that hospital. My mother keeps getting worse, not better. What if Joey somehow knows something about that?"

"I have no idea what you're talking about. Joey had a wonderful experience at his hospital. That's where he was given the mirror box. It was the only thing that could stop his pain after he had to have his arm amputated. We were so grateful."

"Why was his arm amputated?" Isaac asked.

"They said it was bone cancer," Mrs. Haynes replied, but Isaac could hear doubt and uncertainty in her voice. "They ran a lot of tests . . . But it just seemed so strange. How could a young boy like him get bone cancer?"

"Did you get a second opinion?" Isaac asked.

"No. The hospital staff all said they were positive it was bone cancer, and that they needed to act quickly. We had no choice but to let them operate. The doctor told us it was the only hope for him. But that doesn't take away from how tragic it all was. You see, Joey was a pianist—a wonderful one—but you can't really play with only one hand, now can you? One of the staff members managed to find a piece of music for him, though—Ravel's Piano Concerto for the Left Hand. Joey worked so hard at that difficult music, and we just loved to listen to him play. Then his wound got infected, and it spread . . ." Tears were welling up in the woman's eyes. "I have to go now. I'm sorry I couldn't be of more help to you."

"But . . . can I talk to you again sometime? Please? I need to find out as much as I can."

"I don't think that would be a good idea. I have to leave."

And with that she turned and walked away.

Isaac practically shook with frustration on the long ride home. There was something that just didn't sound right to him. It was odd—more than odd—how controlling the hospital had been. Why did they have to operate so quickly after the diagnosis? And why hadn't the Hayneses made a point of getting a second or third opinion about such drastic major surgery? A pit formed in his stomach.

When he got home, Isaac took Vera's red-wine stew and the basil *pistou* out of the freezer. But as he prepared dinner, he couldn't get the day's events out of his mind. He found himself thinking about everything, including the mirror box. He went upstairs and took it out of his closet. Without hesitation, he put his hands in it.

There it was—Joey's hand. It waved at him, then gave a thumbs-up gesture.

But instead of feeling jolted by its presence, Isaac suddenly felt very sleepy, and his eyes drifted shut. His hands were still inside the box. He began to dream. He was standing in a very strange place.

He was surrounded by a hazy mist that made it hard for him to see. The only thing he could make out was a woman standing directly in front of him. She was wearing a bathrobe and staring directly at him as she harshly applied cream to her face, then wiped it off.

Her face was too blurry for him to make out who it was. Her reflection was foggy, like a car window in winter. Isaac wondered if there was a flaw in the mirror. Why was the mirror box showing this to him?

Isaac felt disoriented.

It took him a while to realize where he was.

He was staring at the woman from inside the mirror of her bathroom medicine cabinet.

He had, in a sense, become her reflection.

12

CLEARLY, THE WOMAN COULD NOT SEE HIM. She finished wiping the cream off her face and then studied her reflection. She jiggled the fleshy skin under her chin and pulled on her sagging cheeks. She looked disgusted with herself.

Isaac thought, *She hates the way she looks.*

She also obviously hated the loud rock drumbeats that were pounding through the closed window, making the pane shake. She turned and scowled out the frosted window.

He almost pitied her.

She reached forward and pulled open the door of her medicine cabinet. As she did so, she disappeared from Isaac's view, so that now he was looking at the window. Nothing happened for about a minute, and then the woman swung back into view as she closed the door of the medicine cabinet. Isaac saw her open a container and dump out eight large red capsules. She pulled each of the capsules apart and carefully poured the contents—a white powder—into a small glass bottle.

A name was written on the bottle. Isaac strained his eyes to try to read it, but he couldn't be sure what it said.

Then the woman ran tap water into the bottle and stirred it with her finger until the powder had completely dissolved.

Isaac felt suspended, floating, as though he were looking out from inside an aquarium. He knew that he was inside this woman's bathroom mirror. Was it for real? How could this be happening?

It was Joey Haynes who was showing him this somehow—through the mirror box.

Suddenly, the woman vanished. Isaac was awake and back in his room. He looked at the mirror box.

The phantom limb made a fist—a fist of determination: STOP HER!

13

WAS THE DREAM A SIGN FROM JOEY THAT something at the hospital was very wrong, that someone was tampering with medicine? Isaac didn't understand what was going on, but he didn't like it, especially because he knew Vera could well be in the line of danger. Unless the mirror box had tricked him. Could he trust Joey? He didn't know what to think anymore.

Dinner that night was delicious, what little Isaac actually ate. Grandpa, however, ate more than usual. And he asked a question: "What about that box?"

Isaac was shocked that Grandpa remembered the

box. Perhaps the old Grandpa was returning. He certainly hoped so. He desperately needed to share this nightmare with someone. Could he tell Grandpa about Dr. Ciano, about the box, and about Joey Haynes?

Isaac decided that he would—that he had to—and so he blurted out everything. As he spoke, Grandpa looked at him oddly, apparently confused about what he was hearing. But when Isaac was done, Grandpa followed him upstairs anyway.

In Isaac's room, Grandpa put both of his hands into the mirror box and flexed his right hand.

But all they saw was the reflection of Grandpa's hand. Joey's hand did not appear.

Why wasn't the phantom limb appearing for Grandpa? Isaac was frustrated. Grandpa smiled. "Thanks for showing me your box, Ize," he said.

As soon as Grandpa left the room, the phantom limb appeared in the mirror. It shook a finger at Isaac, as if warning him to keep the box to himself. Then the limb signaled to him: it flashed three fingers twice, then four, and finally five.

Isaac took that to mean that he had better get to the hospital early the next morning, even though he hated being there. But the ominous dream, and now Joey's warning—both of these after having seen Vera's bruise—gave Isaac a sense of foreboding.

The next morning Isaac woke up early. He ignored breakfast, prepared for school, and hopped on his bike.

As usual, the hospital was bustling. Illness doesn't sleep or take holidays. Isaac quickly locked up his bike, entered the hospital, and ran up the stairs.

Outside the intensive care unit, he caught his breath. He was nervous about entering, but there wasn't much time. He checked out the nurses' station from down the hall. He couldn't see anyone, so he proceeded.

He tried to appear relaxed as he approached the nurses' station.

"Did Dr. Ciano leave yet?" he asked a nurse standing by the medication cart.

The nurse—whose pin said VICKY—checked her watch. "I haven't heard."

"Thanks. I'm just going to go pop in on my mother, in six thirty-eight," Isaac said. "If that's OK."

Vicky smiled. "Sure, go ahead. I was on the night

shift. Your mother seemed better, more alert. I talked to her a little bit last night because she had some trouble sleeping."

"Considering her case, that might be good news," Isaac said, feeling relieved. Maybe he didn't have anything to worry about after all.

He pushed open the door to 638. Everything was quiet. The room, dark. Esther, gone. Vera looked up at Isaac as he entered and watched him with a doleful expression. Isaac hated seeing her like this, pale and weak. She looked worse than ever.

Just as he was walking over to her bed, he heard a knock on the door. It was Candi coming in to dress Vera's wound.

Isaac was appalled. "Mom, how are you?" he asked. Then he turned to Candi and said, "What's that bruise on my mother's arm? I noticed it yesterday. It wasn't there when she first checked in. And it's getting huge."

"No. It's very mysterious," Candi said, looking worried. "I'll tell Dr. Ciano again if I see her. I did mark it on her chart."

Vera shrugged hopelessly.

Her personality had again changed, and for the

worse. Isaac was afraid she might be giving up hope of recovery.

Candi smiled. "How come you're here so early?"

"Just stopping by before school," Isaac replied. "Hey, where's Esther?"

"She was dismissed—but that's all I can say," Candi said. When she saw that Isaac was confused, she added, "Sorry, but it's confidential information."

As Candi changed the dressing, Isaac could see that the bruise on his mother's arm was bigger and darker than it was yesterday. Things like this were supposed to get better in the hospital, he thought, not worse.

"Does the doctor know about this bruise?" Isaac asked his mother. "Did she say anything about it?"

"To tell you the truth, I don't remember the last time I saw the doctor," Vera said.

"It's like the nurses do everything and the doctors just make guest appearances," Candi said, and she and Vera chuckled. She finished with Vera's dressing. "Perfect," she said. "I'll be back in the afternoon. Enjoy your visit, Isaac."

After Candi left, Isaac asked Vera, "Do *you* know what happened to your roommate?"

Vera shook her head and looked sad. "All I know is that they moved her out last night. I don't know why."

Isaac was worried, but he had to leave and go to school. And he trusted the nurses.

As he walked past the nurses' station, he saw Candi, who was alone and sitting at the computer. Without looking up, she smiled and said, "Don't worry, Isaac. We know what we're doing here. I'll take good care of her."

14

ISAAC DIDN'T FEEL THE USUAL DREAD AS HE rode toward school. DCynthia had actually helped him the previous day, so maybe the day wouldn't be so bad.

Plus, he had to admit, it was nice to get away from the hospital. He was concerned about Vera, but he felt so uneasy there. School could distract him for a bit.

Isaac saw DCynthia and Destiny approaching. They strolled past him as he was locking up his bike.

"How old is that rattletrap you ride?" Destiny said. "Look at all the other bikes. They're lightweight, and they have twice as many gears as yours."

While Destiny made fun of him, DCynthia fidgeted. She looked away, then shook it off and turned back to him.

"Yeah," she said, joining in. "*Our* father drives us to school in his awesome new Mercedes. He buys a new one every year."

For the first time, Isaac couldn't care less what the twins were saying. He shrugged. "Of course he can afford a car like that," he said. "I bet he makes his money scamming people. I'd be *ashamed* to ride in his car."

They stopped dead in their tracks and stared at each other. For a moment they actually looked shocked.

"What did you just say?" Destiny asked. "You better be on the lookout for Matt Kravetz, twig. He'll take care of a loser like you. No one insults us and gets away with it."

Isaac rolled his eyes. "I'm looking forward to it," he said. "You know, I hate to end this lovely conversation, but it's time for me to get to class. I want to learn something important, not spend my time making people miserable. Maybe you should look into it."

"Mommy's little crybaby!" Destiny chanted.

Isaac fixed his stare on DCynthia until her eyes

dropped down. She didn't look back up. He turned and slowly strolled away. He felt a sense of pride in standing up to them. He had found a little bit more of his own voice.

At lunch, as Isaac sat alone, he was suddenly interrupted by Matt Kravetz. He was holding a tray, so it didn't look as if he wanted to fight. Besides, nobody actually started fights in the cafeteria. Fights took place only if people were so out of control that they didn't care about the consequences. And Kravetz didn't look particularly angry. Still, he dropped his tray onto the table and stood there, hovering over Isaac.

Isaac was nervous, but he figured that he had already stood up to the twins. What could he lose by standing up to Kravetz too? So he looked him squarely in the eyes. "What do you want?" he said.

"Destiny told me what you said to her and DCynthia outside this morning," Kravetz said, leaning forward threateningly.

Isaac shrugged, trying to keep his cool, even though he was clearly nervous. "They're never nice to me," he said. "I was just giving them a taste of their own medicine."

Kravetz seemed taken aback that Isaac was not more intimidated by him.

Isaac went back to eating his tuna sandwich.

Kravetz watched Isaac for a moment, his lips parted, unsure about his next move. He had obviously not been expecting this reaction from him. "Well . . . you just watch it, man," he said, almost as an afterthought.

From the sound of Kravetz's voice, Isaac sensed he had won this encounter.

Kravetz turned and walked away.

After school, Isaac hopped on his bike and started home. As he headed toward the corner, he put on his brakes to slow down, but nothing happened. He tried again. The bike wasn't stopping, and he was zooming straight into the traffic! He started to panic. There was nothing he could do—he was going to collide with a car.

His heart pounding, Isaac knew he had to come up with a plan, and fast. He looked down and realized the only thing he could do was use his feet. He took them off the pedals and dragged them along the ground. It hurt, and he was scared, but he was able to come to a stop just in time.

Sweating and terrified, he got off his bike and

walked unsteadily over to the curb to examine the brakes. He saw that a thick, sturdy twig had been jammed into the place where the brake cable was attached to the wheel. He pulled it out and tested the brakes again. Now they worked.

Isaac was angry. Upset. Furious. And he knew just who to blame. The only ones who could have done this were the twins. They could have killed him! Obviously, DCynthia helping him at the hospital had been some sort of weird fluke. He almost felt like crying.

When he got home, Grandpa was napping on the living room couch. Isaac was still shaken up by his near accident. To calm down, he took a stick of licorice from a jar in the kitchen and went up to the storage room to mess around with his optical illusions. He touched one or two of them, but even as he did that, he was acutely aware of the mirror box. Its allure was irresistible.

He went back to his room, took a bite of the licorice stick, grabbed the mirror box, and put it on his desk. He put the licorice stick down next to the mirror box. Without hesitating, he stuck both forearms into it and looked into the right-hand mirror.

The phantom limb appeared. It made a beckoning

gesture. Instantly, the stick of licorice was *sucked* into the mirror box. Isaac almost jumped out of his chair. How could the mirror box do that?

Then he remembered that the mirror box had already shown him that it had supernatural powers. After all, it was allowing him to communicate with a dead person.

The phantom limb dropped the licorice stick and began pounding on it, hard. Isaac was surprised the mirror box wasn't shaking by the force of it.

He had no idea what the phantom limb was trying to tell him. It was frighteningly clear that Joey was warning him about something—but what?

The next day after school, Isaac went to visit Vera again. Reluctantly, he pushed open the door to the intensive care unit. He was getting tired of spending so much time at the hospital. It seemed to him that things were never going to be normal again— whatever that meant.

He saw Candi sitting at her computer and said hello. Smiling at him, she stood up and followed him into his mother's room.

Vera was asleep. Dr. Ciano was in the room, her

expression somber. "I just got her to rest," she said. "She had trouble sleeping last night."

"Do you know what that bruise on her arm is from?" Isaac asked.

"No, we don't," she said, sighing. "We'll have to do a biopsy." She paused and then turned to Isaac. "Shouldn't you be in school?"

"School's over," Isaac said. It sure seemed that Dr. Ciano didn't want him to be there, that she saw him as a nuisance and not as the son of a very sick patient.

Suddenly, the door opened and a strange but oddly familiar-looking pudgy woman entered the room. For a moment she focused her attention on Vera, then on Isaac. "Oh, excuse me," she said. "I must have the wrong room."

Isaac went over to the sink and turned away from the others to wash his hands. He heard the door open again and two sets of footsteps leave the room.

He hadn't noticed it before, but there was no mirror above the sink.

He barely had time for this to register before he felt someone jab him with a needle.

15

WHEN ISAAC FINALLY AWOKE, HE WAS groggy and bleary-eyed. He knew he was on a gurney—but where? He tried to get off, but he felt too dizzy.

"Whoa, pal!" the orderly said as he wheeled the gurney down the dimly lit corridor.

It was the same dark corridor where Isaac had gotten lost the night Vera was admitted. He didn't like being there. The ceiling was low; the space seemed to close in on him.

As the orderly pushed the gurney around a sharp curve and through a doorway, Isaac saw the sign: ENDOSCOPY. A nurse held the door open.

Inside the small room there were more nurses, all looking cheerful and welcoming. A dark-haired man with a blue mask over his nose and mouth sat at a desk with a computer screen in front of him. The screen did not have a normal display on it, but rather squares with strangely shaped rounded objects inside of them.

The man nodded at Isaac. "Good afternoon," he said. "I'm Dr. Fields. Nice to meet you."

"What's happening?" Isaac asked, feeling more alert. Whatever knockout drug they had given him hadn't lasted very long. Just long enough to trap him here in this awful room.

"You passed out in your mother's room," one of the nurses said. "You were bent over in pain. Thank goodness someone was there to sign the order and send you down here."

"But wait—I'm not a patient," Isaac said. "Someone knocked me out. They gave me a shot with a needle."

"You don't understand how serious this could be," the nurse said. "You need to let us do our job. Doctor's orders."

"But—" Isaac tried to protest.

"Let me explain what we're going to do here today, Isaac," Dr. Fields said. He stood up and walked over to a large black apparatus. He picked up a snakelike object, which was also black. It was thicker at the top end and had concentric bumps on it. "We need to take some pictures of your stomach. This is an endoscope—a camera. I'm going to lower it down your throat and into your stomach, and that's how we'll get the pictures. Do you understand?"

Then Isaac remembered the phantom limb smashing the black licorice. This was what it had been warning him about.

The doctor picked up a small spray bottle. "Don't worry. I'll spray your throat with this anesthetic first. That will make it a lot easier."

The nurses were holding him down now.

"But somebody gave me a—"

"Please try not to scream," Dr. Fields continued. "It makes the procedure more difficult for me. And don't bite down on the camera. It's expensive. Just concentrate on swallowing. That will make it easier for everybody. Open, please," he instructed Isaac.

Isaac pressed his lips together as hard as he could.

"Look, son, we can do this the easy way . . . or the hard way. Open up."

Not knowing what else to do, Isaac opened his mouth. Dr. Fields shot a tiny whisk of spray into his throat and dropped the bottle back into his lab coat pocket. He picked up the endoscope. "OK, let's get going!" he said enthusiastically.

Isaac felt sure that the excitement he heard in the doctor's voice was real and not just in his imagination.

Dr. Fields wedged a hard white plastic cylinder into Isaac's mouth, forcing it to stay open. "This is to keep you from biting down on the expensive equipment," he explained.

Down went the snakelike plastic knob—down past Isaac's uvula, the gagging point. Isaac tried to scream, and then he was hacking and gagging and spluttering. He was in agony.

"Swallow, Isaac," ordered Dr. Fields. "Swallowing will make it easier!"

Isaac tried to swallow, but screaming overcame it.

Meanwhile, Dr. Fields kept pushing the tube down his throat. "Keep swallowing! Keep swallowing!" he said. "It's almost over."

"Yes, yes, it's almost over," the nurses repeated, almost in a chant, holding him down.

Almost over? It looked as if the cable had hardly gone down.

Dr. Fields kept feeding it down with force. Every once in a while he glanced back at the screen and clicked a button, and a picture appeared. "Almost over," he said, grunting.

"Almost over!" the nurses chirped in their sweet little voices, like a chorus from an operetta.

"Almost *over!*" sang Dr. Fields above the sounds of Isaac's agony.

"Almost *over!*" twittered the nurses.

"Just need a couple more snaps now to make sure we got everything. You don't want me to have to do this to you again, do you, son?" Dr. Fields smiled.

He looked back and took another picture.

"Done!" he said.

Finally, Isaac felt him start to pull out the cable. Tears welled up in his eyes.

16

STILL SHAKEN AND CONFUSED BY WHAT HE'D just experienced, Isaac ran out of the hospital as quickly as possible.

On his way out, he passed the woman who had accidentally come into his mother's room just before he'd passed out. She gave him a long look and smiled faintly at him. Then he made the connection. She reminded him of the woman in his dream.

Once outside, he checked the messages on his cell phone. He heard a voice he didn't recognize. "You are asking too many questions," said the voice. Then even more ominously: "Three strikes and you're out."

This sounded nothing like the twins' voices. This was clearly an adult's.

Isaac thought back to his sabotaged bike ride. He wondered if the person who had tampered with his bike could have also jabbed him with the needle.

He looked back at the hospital. He was terrified of ever entering it again, but he knew he had no choice. His mother was still there, possibly in danger, with that growing bruise on her arm.

And now Isaac knew that he was in danger too.

He had no one to turn to except for the only "person" who was actually communicating with him: the phantom limb. Only the phantom limb could help him now.

As soon as he got home, he went upstairs to the mirror box. He wasn't scared of it anymore. Joey Haynes had ripped apart the smiley face . . . and then everybody at the hospital had smiled at him in a strange way. The ripped smiley face had been a warning, he now realized. The licorice stick had been a warning about the endoscopy. So if anyone had any idea of what would happen next, it would be Joey. He was dead, but he was still *some*where. And wherever he was, he obviously had access to information.

Isaac held the mirror box for a moment, then put it on his desk and placed both of his arms into it. Immediately, he felt sleepy.

This time he found himself in a different bathroom mirror. A young teenage girl was reflected in the mirror. Somehow Isaac knew that it was the same person he had seen before. Her face was still blurred, but in his gut, he was sure she was the one Joey showed him earlier.

She was fussing with some rags and a pitcher of some kind of hot liquid, which she held by the handle with one of the rags, like a pot holder. She was muttering to herself, and as her voice grew louder, Isaac could make out what she was saying.

"Those stupid, ugly girls! Why did they put *me* in the same cabin as *them*? They'll get what they deserve for making fun of me. It's not my fault I have a little . . . problem. How can I help it when I'm asleep, anyway?"

She was pouring the hot liquid over the rags.

"The crafts shop won't miss this paraffin for their stupid candle making. The hot water will keep the drain from getting clogged, but so what if it does?" She giggled. "Nobody will even *notice* after what happens to this cabin and those stupid girls."

Isaac knew that paraffin was very flammable. Did she actually want to burn down the cabin?

He could tell her expression was gleeful, but not in a childlike way. There was something about her smile that made him cringe.

Joey must have sensed how much watching this was bothering Isaac, because when Isaac blinked, the girl and the bathroom were gone.

The hand appeared again, holding an instrument that looked like a combination of a saw and a drill. The saw had jagged teeth. When the instrument turned on, the saw blade moved back and forth.

Isaac took his arms out of the mirror box, went over to his computer, and Googled the name that was on the label of the saw. A chill overcame him when he found out what this instrument was for: amputation.

Isaac looked back into the mirror box. The phantom limb dropped the saw and made a fist again. It held the fist there for a minute, shaking it for emphasis.

Isaac was in the way. Dr. Ciano made him feel like an interloper at the hospital. Could she be the one who tampered with the brakes on his bike? If she was, then the endoscopy was only the beginning. Was this newest vision a warning of what could happen to Vera?

He continued to watch the phantom limb. It held up three fingers. Then it slid away but immediately returned with an old green paperback book, *A Collection of Essays* by George Orwell. The author's last name, Orwell, was circled with a very wiggly, scraggly red line. What on earth did *that* mean? What was Joey trying to tell him? It had to have something to do with Vera, but what? Isaac was stumped, though the word "Orwell" sounded vaguely familiar.

"What exactly did you say to DCynthia and Destiny?" Matt Kravetz asked him at lunch the next day. He didn't sit down, but he was less belligerent than the day before.

"They were ragging on me and bragging about their father's car, so I said he's only rich because he cheats people."

"You actually *said* that to them?" A small smile hovered around Kravetz's mouth.

Isaac nodded. He was pleased that Kravetz seemed impressed, and he savored the moment. But it was interrupted when he suddenly made the connection: "Orwell" was the word that DCynthia had whispered when she logged on to the computer at the hospital. Then Joey had told him the same word. It must be a password.

He wondered how he could get his hands on one of the nursing station's computers. Was it possible that there was patient information on the public computers, if you knew the right secret password? He doubted it.

Kravetz noticed that Isaac was preoccupied. "See you later, man," he said, and went over to his friends.

Isaac rode to the hospital directly after school. There were computers at the hospital for visitors to use, for a price. But they offered only the normal Internet. And using them was expensive. He tried one briefly, and then went upstairs to the nurses' station.

Candi was nowhere in sight, and she was not in his mother's room. Vera seemed to be sleeping peacefully, breathing regularly. The bruise on her arm was no bigger than the last time Isaac had seen it. She seemed to be safe for the moment.

The nurses' station was empty, as the other nurses were occupied with taking care of patients in their rooms. The twins were busy running back and forth and didn't seem to notice him. One of the computers faced away from the counter, giving him a chance to use it quickly. Did he dare? When would he have another opportunity?

He typed in "Verdi, Vera." The computer asked for a user name. He tried to type in the name of the hospital, but he was so nervous that he kept making typos. When he finally got the name right, the computer rejected it. He looked over his shoulder to make sure no one was coming. Then he typed in "Ciano." It asked for a password. He typed in "Orwell." A page appeared! He skimmed it rapidly, afraid that at any second a nurse would see what he was doing.

He found the diagnosis quickly. "Patient's biopsy positive for osteosarcoma, bone cancer. Recommendation: amputation."

The same diagnosis that Joey Haynes was given, Isaac thought. This was too much of a coincidence. Dr. Ciano could very well work at more than one hospital and have been Joey's doctor. But then he remembered that the last time he saw Dr. Ciano, she had said they didn't know what was wrong with his mother's arm. So who had recommended the amputation?

He turned off the computer and stepped away from it just in time to see Dr. Ciano herself emerge from a patient's room. Had she seen him at the computer? It was impossible to tell.

She approached the nurses' station. She wasn't smiling now. "Please understand, Isaac," she said. "We care about your mother. She is in good hands. So, really, you don't need to keep coming here all the time."

Isaac left the hospital confused. Obviously, Dr. Ciano didn't want him around. He knew that he had to act fast. Everything that Joey showed him so far had happened, which must mean that something was going to happen with the drill saw too. How soon?

When Isaac got home Grandpa was sitting in the living room reading the newspaper. "How is she?" Grandpa asked him with unexpected clarity.

"The bruise on her arm looks really bad," Isaac replied. Hoping Grandpa would understand, he went on. "Grandpa, do you think . . . you could help me? I think somebody is hurting Mom. Her doctor never wants me around. And yesterday somebody gave me a shot and knocked me out, and I ended up having an endoscopy. They stuck a camera down my throat to my stomach without any sedative—as a warning. It was *horrible*."

Grandpa looked directly into Isaac's eyes. Then he

lifted his head with a look of anger and determination. "We need to get Vera out of there—fast!"

Isaac felt immediate relief at Grandpa's reaction. "Yes, we *have* to," he agreed. "There's an order to amputate Mom's arm. No one told me, but I saw it on the hospital computer."

"How did you get into the hospital computer?" Grandpa said, actually sounding proud of Isaac.

"The phantom limb in the mirror box told me the password, and it was right. Maybe now you'll believe me about that box."

"Amazing," Grandpa said.

It was also amazing to be having a normal conversation with him. Could Grandpa possibly help him? He *had* been a scientist, after all. "I think the dead boy didn't show you his hand because he doesn't want to communicate with anyone but me," Isaac said. "He's also . . . vague. He can't communicate directly. Everything he says is a sign, a puzzle."

He told Grandpa about the Fitzpatrick twins and how they did volunteer work at the hospital. "If I could get them on my side somehow, maybe they could help me."

"You can't control who people like and who they

don't like," Grandpa said. "But you can persuade them."

Isaac knew he was grasping at straws when it came to the twins—they were just too mean, especially Destiny. But maybe there was hope with DCynthia.

"Well, one of them did help me by finding out who lived in this house before us, which is how I found out who the mirror box originally belonged to. And maybe he had the same doctor as Mom, but at a different hospital."

"What about that collection of optical illusions I helped you start a few years ago?" Grandpa asked him. "When was the last time you looked at them? I can't even remember if . . . you moved them here or not." Grandpa seemed embarrassed to admit that.

"I look at them all the time," Isaac said. "Especially the Menger sponge."

"I seem to remember . . . Well, there might be something in that collection that you could use to help you."

Was that really true? Could he trust Grandpa's memory?

If he could, it would be a huge help.

But it was too late to check his collection tonight. He went to sleep instead.

17

AT LUNCH THE NEXT DAY, MATT KRAVETZ actually sat with Isaac instead of with his usual group of friends. It was pretty amazing.

"I can't believe you said that to the twins," he whispered, grinning at Isaac. He was still impressed with what Isaac had said. Clearly, the twins were wrong to think he liked them so much. "Where did you go to school before you came here?" he asked Isaac.

"We used to live in Centerville. Then we moved here." He didn't say that his mother was in the hospital; he didn't want it to sound as if he was asking for sympathy. Instead, he said, "And I found this real cool thing in our new house: a mirror box."

"What's that?" Kravetz asked.

Isaac described the box to him and what you could do with it.

"Hey, man, I'd like to see that sometime," Kravetz said.

"Sure," Isaac said. He didn't say anything about the phantom limb—that would be too unbelievable at this point. But he could tell that Kravetz was fascinated by the idea of the mirror box itself. Isaac decided to work at getting him on his side, so that *maybe* he could help him get the twins on his side too.

And now Isaac felt that he really needed a friend. Not just to help him, but for the companionship.

After school let out, Isaac checked his brakes, just to be sure, and then rode his bike directly home instead of going to the hospital. He knew something strange was going on, but Vera had seemed OK yesterday. And he had to look at his collection of optical illusions again, in case Grandpa was right and there really *was* something he might be able to use to stop whoever it was from hurting Vera—and him.

Grandpa was asleep on the couch when he got home. Isaac wondered if he was tired or if he was slipping back into his disoriented state. Yesterday he had hoped that Grandpa was getting better, that the situation with Vera might be bringing him out of the deep depression he had been in. Because that's what it had been, Isaac suspected now: depression, not dementia.

Isaac went upstairs to look at his collection of illusions. In general, he was most fascinated with the Menger sponge, the cube with the smaller and smaller holes. After toying with it for a minute, he looked up and saw the spiral aftereffect. Why hadn't he noticed it the other day? It was a long rod with a wheel on the end of it. The wheel was white with a black line on it that spiraled into the center. When the wheel turned, it looked as if the spiral was zooming down into the center, pulling you along with it. Then, when you looked away, whatever you saw seemed to be zooming toward you. The effect was dizzying. It was a simple but powerful optical illusion.

He heard footsteps behind him. Grandpa had woken up and followed him upstairs.

"The spiral aftereffect!" Isaac said with excitement.

"That particular model was almost as hard to find as the Menger sponge," Grandpa said, then yawned.

The white disk with the black line spiraling down into it was much bigger than the toy Grandpa had given him when he was five. It was about a foot in diameter. There was a dial with numbers from one to ten on the two-foot-long handle. Isaac picked the spiral aftereffect up, stared at the disk, and turned the dial that made the disk spin—which one you chose determined how fast it went. It turned slowly at first, and he watched as the black line began moving down into the disk, away from him, pulling him along with it. He turned the dial farther, until the disk was spinning faster and faster. Now he felt he was falling into it, and he actually stumbled forward.

"Look away from it now," Grandpa told him.

Isaac followed his instructions. When he looked away, the table seemed to zoom toward him. It was so disorienting that he fell to his knees, closing his eyes for a moment. When he opened them, the table had stopped moving.

"Effective, isn't it?" Grandpa said with a slight smile. "If you stare at a moving object in a particular direction for even a short time, stationary scenes you look at right afterward appear to move in the opposite direction. Some people call it the waterfall effect. If you stare at a waterfall for about a minute, and then look at the rocks at the side of the waterfall, the rocks appear to be moving upward."

It actually made me fall down, Isaac thought.

He couldn't get it out of his mind that he had fallen down after looking at the spiral aftereffect.

Grandpa put his hand to his chin. "Maybe you could use it to your advantage?"

"Yeah!" Isaac said, excited now. "The way I see it, Dr. Ciano must be the one who's ordered the amputation. So maybe I could somehow cause her to have an accident—something that would get her out of the way for a while, which would delay the amputation. That would give us time to get Mom out. Nobody would believe a *toy* could do that. And Grandpa . . . it was all your idea!"

Isaac and Grandpa both started laughing. It wasn't the situation that was funny—they were laughing because they had just solved a problem together. *This is how Grandpa and I used to laugh together before he got sick,* Isaac thought. He realized how much he had missed those times.

There was just one thing missing.

Vera.

18

Aᴼᴛᴇʀ ᴛʜᴇʏ ꜱᴛᴏᴘᴘᴇᴅ ʟᴀᴜɢʜɪɴɢ, Gʀᴀɴᴅᴘᴀ looked around at all the boxes. "There! I knew I made a point of saving the box the spiral aftereffect came in. Good thing nobody was dumb enough to throw it out." He went across the room to get it, and Isaac thought, *I wanted to throw that box out.*

Grandpa handed it to Isaac. "You get the spiral aftereffect and do what you need to do with it . . . I need to take a nap." He was slipping away again. His periods of alertness were sporadic.

In his room, Isaac turned his attention to the mirror box. He wanted to try an experiment using it and the spiral aftereffect. He knew that if the spiral aftereffect appeared in the mirror, Joey Haynes would be able to see it.

Isaac started spinning it inside the box.

The phantom limb slid into the mirror. After a moment it began to shake, as if the spiral aftereffect was making it dizzy. A phantom arm, dizzy? Was it possible? This spiral aftereffect was so large that it took up all of the mirror. Isaac stopped spinning the disk, put it back into his left hand, outside the box, and carefully laid it on his desk. He had wanted to get Joey's reaction to it before he did anything else.

The phantom limb slapped its hand excitedly on the floor of the box, then made a thumbs-up gesture. Isaac knew this meant the phantom limb was very happy now because the trick was something that Isaac had discovered on his own and showed to Joey.

Isaac withdrew his hand from the box. The phantom limb held up three fingers. It made an OK sign with its thumb and index finger, waved happily, and disappeared.

Isaac sat on his bed with the spiral aftereffect and began studying it more closely. He had to understand exactly how to spin it at the right speed to make the right effect.

Looking at the numbers on the disk, he began turning the dial. At one, it spun quite slowly, and there was not much of an effect. At two, he began to see the line slide slowly down inside the disk. He went up to four, and now the line was really spinning down inside it. Isaac dared to turn it all the way up to ten. The effect was so strong that it pulled him right off the bed.

He quickly looked around the room. Everything in his room was converging toward him. It was as though the whole room was about to crush him. The feeling was very real, all because the spiral aftereffect took up his whole field of vision. The speed at ten would have to be used against the person who was endangering Vera and himself, he decided. The sensation would easily knock someone over.

When the sensation stopped, Isaac put the spiral aftereffect into its box and went back to the mirror box again. He felt sleepy.

He knew what was coming.

But this time he was looking into a different bath-room, not clean and white and perfect like the first one or rustic like the second. There was old-fashioned wallpaper and a flowered shower curtain. The linoleum on the floor was worn. And there was nobody in the room.

Then he heard the door open and, a moment later, the lock click. A young girl appeared in the mirror, holding up a plastic baby doll that was about eight inches long. Its clothes had been removed.

The little girl was so short that only her head and her arms with the doll appeared in the mirror. Her face was still blurred.

"Bad baby! I told you not to do that," she said so softly that Isaac could barely hear her. She had locked the door and now she was whispering: she didn't want her parents to know what she was doing in there. "Bad, *bad* baby!" she said again. Then, with her tongue pushed slightly out of her mouth, she began twisting one of the doll's arms. She twisted the arm around backward and pulled at it, grunting slightly. There was a slight crack, but the arm remained attached. She kept pulling, harder and harder, until the arm was at right angles to the doll's body. With one final burst of effort, she snapped the arm off.

The little girl beamed, as happy as if it were

Christmas morning. She dropped the severed arm into the sink. "Oh, my dear little baby," she suddenly cooed as she lovingly rocked the doll, "Mommy will make everything OK now."

Isaac was shocked by the little girl's cruelty and then by her elation. The image faded, and he was looking into the mirror box again. The phantom limb had returned and was trying to tell him something. It held up three fingers, as it had done before, and shook them at Isaac.

"Three?" Isaac said out loud.

The phantom limb shook in disagreement. It held up three fingers again.

Isaac tried again. "Third?" It made him think of the games of charades his parents had sometimes played at their dinner parties. From upstairs, he had listened to them guessing and laughing. This, however, was deadly serious.

"Three's company?" Isaac suggested.

The limb shook itself in exasperation.

What on earth was the limb trying to say? Everything the phantom limb had shown him so far was important, so this must be important too. He would have to figure out its meaning in relation to the little girl—whoever she was—and her amputation of her doll's arm.

He quickly pulled his hands out of the mirror box. The phantom limb folded its fingers down over its palm in a sorrowful gesture, and left. Isaac put the box in the closet right away.

He went downstairs to do something about dinner. Grandpa was not asleep on the couch, as Isaac had expected. Instead, he was looking at a copy of *Scientific American*. Isaac told Grandpa what the phantom limb had done, how it was trying to tell him something. He also told him about the "mirror dream" he had just had.

"But it's not 'three,' 'third,' or 'three's company,'" he said.

"Hmm . . ." Grandpa squeezed his eyes shut for a moment, thinking hard. "Well, it could be 'triptych.' Or 'troika.' Maybe even 'triad,'" he suggested.

"What's a triad, exactly?" Isaac asked.

"I . . . I seem to remember it might mean two different things," Grandpa said. "I think it could be a musical term for a particular three-note chord."

"Well, Joey Haynes *did* play the piano," Isaac said. "But how could that connect with the little girl mutilating her doll? What's the other meaning of triad?"

"Any group of three, like three closely related people."

"I wonder if that's what the phantom limb meant. But *which* three people? It still doesn't make a lot of sense."

Grandpa shook his head and sighed. "I can't stop thinking about that little girl and her doll. Whoever that girl is, she's sick—and dangerous. We've got to get your mother home. Fast."

Isaac knew that. But he still didn't know how he was going to zap Dr. Ciano with the spiral aftereffect. When—and how? He had to catch her off guard, so she'd injure herself and have to be away from work for a while. But everybody at the hospital was so vigilant. The whole idea seemed impossible.

And he wondered: Who was the woman who had "accidentally" come into Vera's room? Why had she smiled at him so strangely when she saw him right after the endoscopy? It was almost as if she knew what had happened to him.

After dinner was over and he was back in his room, he puzzled over the whole situation as he sat at his desk, trying to concentrate on his homework. He was falling way behind in his schoolwork and would probably fail his upcoming tests. But he couldn't concentrate on any of it. All he could think about was how he could use the spiral aftereffect and get Vera out of the hospital before anything really terrible happened to her.

He remembered the sensation of his own room closing in on him. It had been very scary. Escaping from a room that was getting smaller and smaller made him think of something else he had seen in his collection: the Menger sponge—the cube that was made out of holes and had infinite surface area and zero volume. If you were inside it, every space you entered would be smaller than the one you had left.

His head began to nod. It was only nine thirty in the evening, but he'd had a long and eventful day. Maybe if he went to bed now he could get up early and concentrate on his homework then. He undressed, turned off the overhead light, and got into bed. He tried to read a little more, but his eyes kept slipping shut. The book dropped out of his hand. He fell asleep with the reading light on.

And then he had a dream. He was in Vera's room at the hospital. But the room had no window. A fire was burning in the wastebasket. Bright flames jumped from the wastebasket and ran up the curtains next to the bed. Vera was lying in the bed, asleep. She was drugged again. Isaac remembered the little girl he had seen in his mirror box dream and the way she had seemed to be preparing to start a fire.

In his dream, Isaac tried the door. It was locked. Someone had started the fire and then locked them in the room.

He looked up frantically. On the blank wall he could see the Menger sponge. He pushed his hand against the wall. His arm went through it easily. He could go into the Menger sponge! The room there would be smaller, but it would not be on fire. He had to pull Vera into the Menger sponge and out of the burning room.

He lifted Vera out of the bed. She was as light as a feather. He slung her over his shoulder and moved toward the wall, one arm holding her, the other held in front of him. His arm went right through the wall. They were going to get out!

But when Vera's leg touched the wall, it wouldn't go through. Isaac had access to the Menger sponge, but Vera's inert body didn't. Vera was trapped in the room. He couldn't save her. He felt the flames against the back of his legs. Vera's hair was engulfed in flames now. He pushed her against the wall again and again, but she couldn't fit through it. They were both going to burn to death.

At that moment, he woke up. Luckily, he managed not to scream and wake up Grandpa. He lay in his bed panting, still filled with the horror of the dream.

The nightmare had been bizarre and terrifying. But it still meant something. It was telling him, with more force than ever, what he already knew: he had no time, and he had to act now.

He was wide awake and anxious. He knew he wouldn't be able to get back to sleep. He looked at his watch. It was four thirty A.M. He had to make a plan for using the spiral aftereffect. He had to do it today, after what he had just seen in his dream. He had to use the spiral aftereffect on whoever had put in the amputation order—Dr. Ciano or whoever was responsible. He had to get to the hospital.

Where, he figured, more trouble would be waiting for him.

Isaac skipped breakfast and went directly to the hospital. He didn't see Candi at the nurses' station. It must still be the night shift. He went to Vera's room and found that she was sleeping. He wanted to get out as quickly as possible, but he felt he should stay and try to learn more. He began washing his hands. He thought he heard muffled footsteps. But before he even had a chance to look, he was jabbed again, and darkness slammed down on him.

This time he woke up sooner—he was still in the elevator. This one wasn't so small. It was big enough to hold a gurney. He struggled to sit up and look. He could see that the button for the basement was lit. When the elevator doors opened, the orderly pulled the gurney into the small dark corridor he hated so much.

"What's happening?" Isaac asked, his voice rising in panic. After the endoscopy, he knew this was going to be torture.

"MRI," the orderly said, not explaining what that meant. "Here we are."

The door that said MRI led to a suite. In the first room the orderly, who was tall and strong, helped him off the gurney and motioned to a desk. The woman behind the desk handed Isaac a form on a clipboard.

Isaac threw the clipboard to the floor. "There's nothing wrong with me!" he said. "Someone's trying to hurt my mother and get back at me."

The orderly thrust the clipboard back at Isaac. "I'll stand here all day until you sign this."

Reluctantly, his hands shaking, Isaac signed the form.

The orderly did not leave—he was going to be there throughout the procedure, Isaac guessed, to keep him from escaping.

A man in a white lab coat emerged from an inner doorway. "Come with me," he said. "First the locker room, where you change into a hospital johnny and lock up your clothes and valuables—your wallet, your watch, your keys, everything. Then across the hall to the MRI machine."

"This is crazy!" Isaac shouted. "Who's responsible for this? I said there's nothing *wrong* with me."

The man shrugged. "Orders from upstairs. We do what they say. This way, please."

Isaac knew the hospital was short-staffed and that people were always rushing around and taking care of hundreds of patients. It would be easy for someone to sabotage a single patient.

Isaac wanted to run for it. He was sweating. But the orderly was right there.

The locker room was small, the lockers half-sized. The man left him alone after telling him the instructions, but the orderly stayed. Isaac took off his clothes and stuffed them into one of the small lockers. He had a terrible sinking sensation. This was going to be bad. He knew it.

The room across the hall had a control panel and a large window looking into the adjoining room, which contained a metal cylinder big enough for a person. Isaac couldn't help thinking of a coffin. "You just go in there and the nurse will help you," the man said. He was seated at the control panel. The orderly stood beside him, watching Isaac closely.

Isaac dragged himself into the room, his eyes focused on the metal cylinder. There was a hole in it big enough to go through, and a gurney to lie down on coming out from the hole. There was no doubt in his mind—he was going to have to go inside that cylinder.

He panicked. He felt as if he was going crazy.

"I . . . I don't have to go *inside* that thing, do I?" he asked the nurse, trying to keep his voice from shaking.

And then he recognized her. She was the odd woman who had "accidentally" come into Vera's room, the same one who had smiled strangely at him after the endoscopy. What was she doing here? Was she part of what Isaac was beginning to feel was a conspiracy against him? Maybe the mystery woman and Dr. Ciano were in this together. And could there possibly be another person involved . . . making it a "triad"?

She smiled and touched his arm, as if she had known him for a long time. "It's only for twenty minutes. Most people have no trouble at all. Just try not to move a single muscle so we can get some good pictures . . . or else we'll have to do it again. Now, just lie down here." She patted the gurney attached to the machine. The pillow for his head was right at the opening in the machine.

"I have to go in *head first*?" Isaac said, trembling.

The nurse smiled. "Just lie down here and get comfortable."

Isaac could barely stifle a groan. He lay down on the gurney with his head on the pillow, his heart thumping so loudly it seemed to fill the room.

The nurse took some little rubber things and inserted them into his ears. "Earplugs. The machine gets a little noisy. Ready now?"

Isaac wanted to answer, "Not on your life," but how could he get away now? He could see the orderly, still guarding him, through the large window over the control panel in the next room. It was the only way out.

The nurse pressed a button somewhere. The gurney began sliding slowly into the cylinder. Every second Isaac felt his panic rising. He wanted to kick and scream, but if he moved, they'd have to do it all over again. He had no idea how much time was going by and how soon it would be over.

He'd been inside the thing for only a few seconds and already sweat was sliding down his forehead into his eyes, making them sting. But he couldn't move his arm to wipe it away. He tried not to hyperventilate, so his chest wouldn't move. He felt that at any second he was going to have a seizure, like Vera, or scream, or throw up.

Why hadn't they offered to give him something to knock him out? It felt exactly the same as when they hadn't given him a sedative for the endoscopy.

Then there were noises all around him, weird, unearthly noises unlike anything he had ever heard before. Deep rumbling, like thunder, turning into a high-pitched screeching that penetrated painfully through the plugs in his ears. He held his body as tightly as possible, feeling the sweat oozing down his sides now. Soon his hospital gown was soaking wet and his eyes were stinging more than ever. It felt as if he'd been in here for hours.

"Only fifteen minutes left," a voice said through a loudspeaker inside the machine.

Fifteen more minutes? How could he stand this? He squeezed his eyes shut, so he wouldn't see how close the top of the cylinder was. He desperately needed to stifle the painful stinging. He did everything he could to imagine he was somewhere else. But all that came into his mind was the Menger sponge, the strange fractal object in which every chamber was smaller than the one before. And that only made it worse.

He tried to think of riding his bike, of trees and the sky. But the Menger sponge kept swimming back into his mind. His muscles were aching now from holding them so rigidly. It felt like hours were going by in this hell. How could he take this? How *could* he? How—

The noises stopped. And finally, *finally,* the gurney began sliding out of the cylinder.

Isaac was a wreck. He was so limp, the nurse had to help him climb down off the gurney. The man in the white lab coat told the orderly to get a wheelchair and then took Isaac into the locker room, where, with shaky hands, Isaac slowly got into his clothes.

As the orderly wheeled him to the elevator, Isaac gradually began to recover. He knew that the more he hung around the hospital, trying to figure out what was really going on, the more they would find ways to torture him.

He and Vera had to escape tomorrow.

19

ISAAC GOT TO THE HOSPITAL EARLIER THAN ever the next day, at six. He felt shaky about going there at all, afraid of what they might do to him this time, but he knew he had to force himself to go. He was getting more and more worried about Vera.

He brought the spiral aftereffect with him, carefully wrapped and taped in its box, the box itself wrapped in a towel. He fitted it snugly into his bicycle basket. His schoolbooks and unfinished homework weighed down his backpack as he rode.

Nurse Vicky was at the station. "Is the doctor here yet?" Isaac asked her.

Vicky checked a chart on the wall behind her. "The doctor doesn't get here this early."

"Is Candi here?" Isaac asked.

"Candi changed shifts today. She's in the ER and won't be up on this floor at all," she said, smiling pleasantly.

Did Vicky know what was happening to Vera? Could Isaac trust her? He wasn't sure, so he continued on to room 638 without saying anything more.

Isaac found Vera awake, staring at the ceiling. She was looking worried and vulnerable. She seemed more alert than she had been in the last few days. Was it because Dr. Ciano wasn't there to dope her into submission? When she saw Isaac in the doorway, her pale, shrunken face broke into a big smile. "Ize! Where've you been?"

"I've been here. But you've just been asleep—drugged out," he said as he washed his hands.

"I want to go home, Ize."

"I'm working on it, Mom. We'll get you home. Grandpa's even been helping me around the house, can you believe it?"

He walked over to the bed. He felt a chill when he saw that there was a bigger, thicker bandage on her arm where the bruise was. Was the bruise larger and deeper now? His mind flashed back to the little girl and her doll. Was someone purposefully enlarging the bruise while Vera was knocked out?

Isaac sat down in a chair next to the bed. He tried to sound as calm as possible. "I got the password for the hospital computer, and I went on to look up your records. I saw . . . something bad. Do you think you can handle it?"

Vera sat up straight. "Yes, I have to know." She took a deep breath. "What did you see?"

"Somebody's written a bogus report. It says that you have bone cancer. They want to amputate your arm—the one with the bandage on it."

Vera's face froze. "But that's . . . that's . . . How can they do that?" Her voice rose almost to a wail.

"It's what happened to the kid who had the mirror box, and now they've got you. Have you seen the doctor *at all* since that day when I was here?"

"Candi said that Dr. Ciano's been in to check on me, but I've always been asleep."

"Don't trust anyone, Mom," Isaac said. "I'm going to stop them, and you'll be safe."

"I think they took something out of my arm, where the bruise is," Vera went on shakily. "I must have been asleep when they did it. I noticed because blood was seeping out from under the bandage when I woke up. All Candi said, when she fixed the bandage, was that it was for a biopsy—a biopsy for bone cancer?" She sounded really scared now.

Isaac reached out and gently touched her hand. "Mom, I'm sure you don't have bone cancer. Somebody here is demented. They're lying. They must have switched your biopsy results with another person who really *does* have bone cancer. Grandpa and I are going to stop them. And we have a plan—a good plan." He wasn't going to tell her what the plan was. She wouldn't understand the spiral aftereffect.

"Oh, Ize," Vera said. But luckily she didn't ask him about the plan. She looked down and bit her lip, as if trying to hold back tears. "Do you remember my former roommate here, the doctor named Esther?" she asked Isaac, her voice breaking.

"Yes," Isaac said.

"Before she left, she was telling me that she remembered a girl from somewhere, and it was a bad memory. Before they knocked her out and took her away, the memory came back to her," Vera said. "And she told me." She took a deep breath. "Years ago, Esther took a job as the doctor at a summer camp. There was a girl at the camp, about thirteen years old, who had a lot of problems and no friends. She wet the bed, and the other girls made fun of her for it. Then some of the other girls' things started to go missing. They told one of the camp counselors, who sent her to Esther. Esther tried to tell the girl not to pay attention to the taunts of the other girls, but she could tell the girl's problems were deep. She wrote a letter to the girl's parents suggesting that the girl see a therapist after she got home from camp."

Isaac remembered the vision the phantom limb had shown him of the girl in a rustic bathroom, planning to start a fire, and muttering about the other girls. "What else did Esther say?" he asked her urgently.

Sounding almost like her old self, Vera continued, "A little while later, the cabin where that girl was staying burned down. The other girls were in there when it happened. One of them got pretty badly burned. Esther had to call for an ambulance and get her to the nearest hospital. The troubled girl wasn't in the cabin when it happened. She disappeared for hours. When they found her, she was hysterical. She swore that she was only making candles to give to the other girls as presents, so they would like her. But Esther didn't believe her. The girl's demeanor quickly changed to blankness. Esther knew there was something really wrong with the girl."

"What else?" he said to Vera.

"The girl was safely outside the cabin when the fire happened."

It all fit together, horribly. The girl had been damaged and dangerous since childhood. Isaac had a sudden flash of insight. "She . . . must really hate people. And I have a feeling she really doesn't like people who play the piano. She used to torment her dolls and pull their limbs off."

"How could you possibly know that?" Vera asked him, her voice despairing.

"It's a long story. It has to do with what I learned from Joey Haynes, the boy who had the mirror box."

"But he's dead! How could you—"

"I mean, from his grandmother. I went to see her. She lived in our house before we did. She told me a lot." That was a lie, but it was something that Vera might believe more easily than what he had seen in the mirror box. "Joey Haynes played the piano, like you."

Vera looked scared. "I just want to get out of here, now," she said.

Isaac glanced at the open door of her room. He

turned and said, "I know you can't walk, so we'll have to use a wheelchair. The other nurses *seem* nice, but I don't know. We should play it safe and come up with a story. We could say we're just taking a little ride around the hospital to get you some air—and then escape."

Vera held up her hands, showing him the IV lines, which were inserted with a needle and secured by bandages. As before, the IV lines were attached to a tall metal pole that had bags hanging from it. "If we were going to leave the hospital, we'd have to remove all of this. Nobody would let out a patient on an IV."

"Maybe we could find a bathroom and take it out ourselves. You can ride in a wheelchair while you're attached to the bags. I'll ask Vicky if we can get one," Isaac said, his heart beginning to beat faster.

"Ask her now, please!"

Isaac went out to the nurses' station and found Vicky. "My mother feels so much better today," he told her. "But she's getting achy from lying in bed all the time. Would it be possible for us to take a little ride around inside the hospital? Just for a change of scenery?"

Vicky looked both worried and apologetic. "My instructions are to keep her on complete bed rest," she said with a sigh. Isaac sensed she was questioning her instructions.

"Oh, come on," Isaac pleaded. "Please? She really needs to get out of that room."

"If I let her out of her room, I'll lose my job," Vicky said.

"Says who?"

Vicky hesitated. "Dr. Ciano and Candi," she said softly. "They're my superiors. If I don't follow their instructions to the letter, I'm out of here—with no recommendations and no possibility of getting another job. I just can't risk it. Your mother's condition is too unstable because of her arm."

Isaac's shoulders slumped. He turned and went back to Vera's room. "There's no way they'll even let you out of the room. *All* the nurses will stop us."

Vera bit her lip, trying to hold back tears.

So they couldn't get out now. There would have to be another plan. Isaac looked at his watch. It was six forty-five already. He needed to get to school early—with the spiral aftereffect. "I promise we'll get you out of here before anyone can do anything else bad to you," he said. "Grandpa's helping me." He brightened a little. "He's almost the way he used to be. He remembers things. He might be in here to see you today—I got up before he did, but maybe he'll come."

"Please get me out of this place, Ize, but please be careful."

"Mom, I have a plan. I think you'll be safe today," Isaac said. He put on his backpack and picked up the spiral aftereffect. "Bye. I'll be back later."

Now the really hard part was about to begin.

20

As Isaac rode to school, he tried to imagine the day ahead. He had decided, after waking up so early, that he should test the spiral aftereffect on somebody else before using it on someone at the hospital. Doing it to himself alone was not enough of a test. But who could he use it on? He would have loved to try it on Destiny, but she would definitely tell someone and ruin the whole plan. The only other person he could think of was Matt Kravetz—he was the closest thing Isaac had to a friend here. Kravetz had seemed fascinated when Isaac told him about the mirror box, which meant he was likely to find the spiral aftereffect amazing too.

Isaac got to school at seven fifteen, fifteen minutes before the first bell. As he locked up his bike, he spotted some boys fooling around with a football, throwing it back and forth. Real football practice was after school. These were the dedicated athletes, the ones who got to school early to hone their skills even more. One of them was Kravetz. Isaac didn't want to waste any time. Now would be a great time to start his plan.

He walked as close to the group as he could without being in the way and took the spiral aftereffect out of its box. He pointed it in the direction of the boys and began running it on level four.

For a while—it seemed like forever to Isaac—none of them noticed it, they were so involved in their game. Then one guy, who had stopped for a moment to tie his shoe, looked up and saw it. He stood up and stared at it, so transfixed that he couldn't return to the game. The disk was big enough to create the effect at a distance. Someone threw the ball at him to get his attention, but he didn't notice the ball was coming until the last second and he missed it.

"Hey, what's the matter with you, Lupton?" somebody shouted at him.

Lupton didn't respond. He was still watching the

spiral aftereffect. Other guys turned to look too, including Kravetz.

"I'm out for a minute," Kravetz called, and he strolled over to Isaac, his eyes on the spinning disk. When he got close, he shook his head and chuckled. "What is it with you?" he said, still staring at the spiral aftereffect. Isaac speeded it up to seven. "First you tell me about that weird mirror box thing, and now you show up at school with this . . . whatever it is—which seems to hypnotize people. Are you into magic tricks or something?"

"Science," Isaac said. "Look at it again, then look away from it and see what happens."

Kravetz looked at the spiral aftereffect for a few moments more, then at the school building. He stumbled but didn't quite fall. Isaac could imagine what he was seeing: the school building coming toward him. If he had set it at level ten, it would have been zooming.

Kravetz turned and looked directly at Isaac, ignoring the other boys, who were waiting around for him. "Wow! *That* was amazing," he said breathlessly. "What the hell happened? Why did the school start moving toward me?"

"Motion aftereffect," Isaac said. "If you stare at

something moving steadily in one direction for a while and then turn away and look at something stationary, what you're looking at seems to move in the opposite direction."

He explained about the waterfall effect and ended by saying, "Cool, isn't it?"

Some of the other guys had come over out of curiosity and were standing next to Kravetz now.

"What *is* that thing?"

"What's it for?"

"Why did you bring it to school?"

"Show-and-tell," Isaac answered sarcastically.

The boys laughed at his joke, and Isaac felt a sense of relief—he had actually made them laugh.

"OK, back to practice," Kravetz announced. "Or I'll tell coach on you. There are still a few minutes left."

The other boys dispersed. And when they started running and passing the ball around again, they seemed to forget about Isaac and his peculiar device.

"Why *did* you bring it to school?" Kravetz asked him.

"Well . . . I wanted to show . . . I thought you might be . . . Listen, man," Isaac blurted out, "I really need your help."

"With what?"

"The twins," Isaac told him. "They could help me and my mother at the hospital. Aren't you friends with them?"

"I want them to *think* I'm their friend," Kravetz said, looking embarrassed. "I sure don't want them to be my enemies. I've seen what they can do." He looked down, averting his eyes. Then he looked up at Isaac again. "Why do you want me to help you with them?"

Isaac looked at his watch. "It's a long story. No time to tell you now."

The bell rang.

"Maybe I'll see you at lunch," Kravetz said, and Isaac felt better. He could tell him the whole story then.

He returned the spiral aftereffect to its box, and once he was inside the school he carefully put it in his locker.

He waited impatiently through his morning classes. Several teachers spoke to him privately after class, telling him he was falling behind in his homework and warning him that if he didn't get it together he'd be in danger of failing. Isaac tried to explain that his mother was in the hospital and that he'd get back on track when she was better. Some of the teachers seemed sympathetic, but others were more demanding.

The fact of the matter was, Isaac couldn't care less. Right now school was the least of his worries.

At lunch, he sat by himself, as usual. The difference was that today he genuinely hoped Kravetz would join him. He needed Kravetz to help him with his plan. Time was running out. It seemed possible that he might help, now that Isaac knew how Kravetz really felt about the twins.

But he also wanted Kravetz to eat with him because he wanted to be his friend. Joking around with him earlier had reminded Isaac of how nice it was to be around someone his own age.

And then Kravetz was standing at his table with his tray. He sat down across from Isaac. "I don't know why you want me to help you with those two," Kravetz said. "Especially Destiny."

Isaac's heart lifted. "It's a long story," he said. "I'll try to be quick about it."

"All right, but hurry. You know how short lunch period is," Kravetz said.

"You'll be surprised," Isaac said, and plunged in. He quickly described Vera's original symptoms and how Dr. Ciano, Candi, and possibly others were keeping his mother sedated most of the time, giving her lots of drugs. Instead of getting better, his mother's condition was worsening. He recounted what Esther, Vera's roommate, had said about a girl at camp, and how quickly Esther had been moved away. He told him what he had learned from Joey Haynes's grandmother—that they hadn't liked his doctor, and how the boy had ended up first one-armed and then dead. Whoever was doing this seemed to be fixated on piano players—Joey and his mother and also the girl's brother. This person had dismembered her dolls when she was a child.

Kravetz seemed fascinated, but he was clearly also confused. "How do you know all this?" he asked.

Isaac realized that if he told Kravetz about the phantom limb, Kravetz would think he was hallucinating and immediately discount the whole story. So he simply said, "When Esther worked at that camp, she found some of the girl's mutilated dolls. I've got to get my mother out of there before that happens to her."

"What about the doctor?" Kravetz wanted to know.

"Whenever the doctor's there, my mother's asleep

or unconscious. And somebody tampered with the lab results so it looks like my mother has bone cancer. The doctor can easily log in whatever lab results she wants. My mother has a big sore on her arm that's getting worse, and it wasn't there at all when she entered the hospital."

Kravetz sighed and shook his head. "Geez, it sounds pretty bad," he admitted. "But I still don't get why you want the twins on your side."

"You didn't know they have to volunteer at the hospital? Community service, I think—as punishment for something they did." Isaac shrugged. "But I don't know for sure."

"Oh, I know. They were caught shoplifting," Kravetz said. "So what do you expect *them* to do to help get your mother out of there?"

"I'm not sure," Isaac replied, shrugging again. "But I know that they know their way around the hospital and that they have access to places I can't get to. If they were on my side, it would be three instead of just one against the hospital staff. And the twins *are* pretty good at being sneaky."

The bell rang.

Kravetz stood up and picked up his tray. "I don't

know what I can do about the twins—you know how they can be." He thought for a few seconds. "If . . . if you spin that spiral thing faster, does it—"

"It can make people fall down. That's what I want to do to the people who are hurting my mother at the hospital—incapacitate them so I can get my mother away from there. But it has to be at the right time and the right place, so it will really have an effect. That's where the twins come in."

Kravetz's eyes widened. "You have the nerve to do that?" He sounded impressed. "Listen, I'll try to get them to cooperate. I'll see if I can find out how they feel about the hospital. But I can't say too much. They have big mouths, you know. Meet me at the bike rack after school."

Isaac smiled and nodded in agreement.

21

ISAAC HURRIED TO THE BIKE RACK AFTER HIS last class. He was sick of the guilt trips he was getting from teachers. Kravetz wasn't there yet. He unlocked his bike and waited impatiently. He wanted to hear how it had gone with the twins, but he also wanted to get to the hospital as soon as possible to make sure Vera was safe.

Finally, Kravetz came out of the school building and jogged toward him. He reached the bike rack and got right to the point. "Sorry. Out of luck, pal. The twins wouldn't listen to me about you. They have this fixation. They said they're having too much fun messing with you. If I keep trying to convince them that you're cool, then they might turn on me." He shrugged.

What else could he say? More and more it was becoming clear that Kravetz really was a decent guy, and interested in some of the same things Isaac was, despite being a jock.

"Well, thanks for trying. I'll . . . see what I can do on my own. Maybe I can change their minds."

"Maybe," Kravetz said, with no emotion in his voice. "I have to get to practice. Sorry again." He jogged away from Isaac.

Isaac checked his bike for any more tampering, hopped on, and rode away quickly. Now he was worried about Kravetz as well as everything else. Why had he become so cold all of a sudden? Had Isaac told him too much? But he had to push that out of his mind and stay focused. His priority right now had to be to win over DCynthia. He didn't have much hope about Destiny.

The twins were seated at the desk at the entrance to the intensive care unit, checking visitors' IDs. "We were expecting you, tool," Destiny said with a smirk.

"Don't you have a life?" DCynthia said, but she had

a guilty expression as she said it. At least her voice was soft, not braying. They both had to be careful that the staff didn't hear them taunt a visitor.

"Why did you think Matt would ever help someone like *you?*" Destiny asked. She put her hand over her mouth and giggled. DCynthia looked away. When Destiny got her laughter under control, she continued smugly, "We told him to shut up about you. And it worked."

Isaac had to fight the urge to smack her. It had been a vain hope to think he could get them on his side, but he had to try one more time. "What about Dr. Ciano?" he said. "What do you think of *her?*"

"We know how to play everybody here so we get what we want, not like the other candy stripers. The staff gives us the easiest jobs, like sitting here and checking in guests. We've talked to some of the other candy stripers. They're always running around getting exhausted. *That's* not for *us!* We're getting out of here as soon as our time is up. *Hasta la vista.*"

He sighed and gave up. "Gotta go check on—"

"Your *mommy!*" Destiny mocked him.

Candi was at the nurses' station. "I'm afraid your mother won't have much to say to you today, dear," she said pleasantly. She clucked her teeth and shook her head. "I have to tell you that the doctor's very worried about her."

He wanted to say, *None of you seem worried about her.* Instead, he controlled himself and said determinedly, "I need to see her."

"I'm afraid you can't," Candi replied. She smiled at him. "She's going to have a procedure in the basement soon."

He felt scared, but he was determined to fight back. "It'll just be for a minute. OK?"

Candi's voice had a steely edge to it. "Well, all right. You can open the door and peek in for a few seconds."

As he feared, Vera was unconscious. The bandage on her arm was even larger than before. Her body seemed almost lifeless. There was no more time.

Isaac rushed home and immediately got out the mirror box. He needed the phantom limb's help before it was too late.

The phantom limb slid into the mirror. It was holding up three fingers again. Was it really trying to say "triad," as Grandpa had suggested? Isaac knew he had to search the net to find out what Joey was trying to tell him.

Grandpa had known only two meanings for the word, the musical term and the group of three people. How could he find out if it had any other meaning?

He went downstairs and found Grandpa reading. He asked him about the term "triad" for the second time. After thinking about it, Grandpa said, "If it refers to that doctor, maybe it has something to do with psychology."

Isaac went back upstairs, opened his computer, and went to Google. He typed in "triad and psychology." Several entries appeared with the title "Macdonald Triad."

"Yes!" Isaac said to himself. He'd found it!

"The triad" referred to three childhood behaviors that were often displayed by children with psychopathic tendencies who were prone to becoming serial killers. Most kids with one, or even two, of these behaviors never became a serial killer. But almost every serial killer who had ever been studied possessed all three. One trait was cruelty to animals or other small creatures—like the way the girl in the mirror treated her dolls. Another trait was enuresis, or bed-wetting, which was why the other girls in the cabin had made fun of her. The third trait was arson, the deliberate starting of fires. If Isaac had ever seen someone look happy, it was when that girl was preparing to burn down the cabin—with the other girls in it.

He went over to the mirror box again. He wrote down two questions. "Did that woman kill other people before she killed you? Does she want to kill my mother?" He held the piece of paper so that it was reflected in the mirror.

The phantom limb didn't merely read the paper, it *sucked* it into the mirror box. It had done the same thing with the licorice. How was that possible? How was any of this possible? He would have to do research on mirror boxes as soon as he could. Forget about homework—this was more important.

The phantom limb reappeared. It gave a vigorous thumbs-up, meaning the answer to both questions was yes. Isaac felt more scared than ever now that he had found out about the triad and had seen that look on the girl's face as she prepared to burn down the cabin with the girls in it. Horror stories about famous serial killers bombarded his mind, the things they did to their victims before and after killing them. How some kept severed heads and other body parts in their fridges. It terrified Isaac to think he was dealing with some kind of sociopath.

He had to tell Grandpa, so he hurried down to the kitchen.

Grandpa was bent over the oven. "I was about to call you to come down and eat," he said. "The steaks are just done."

Isaac was shocked. It had been months since Grandpa had cooked a meal. But he didn't want to say anything about it—he didn't want to do anything that might interfere with his progress. "Thanks, Grandpa," he said, "but I'm too worried to eat much. There really *is* a serial killer at the hospital. Whoever killed Joey Haynes has killed other people. And Mom is next. Besides the doctor, there's another suspicious woman there too. We'll have to sneak Mom out. I don't know any other way to get her discharged."

"Isaac, we can do it," Grandpa said. "But you have to calm down. We can't accomplish anything if you're in a panic."

Isaac sighed. "I'll try. But it's not easy after all that's happened—to her *and* to me."

"Just get control of yourself. We have to be precise about our plan. I went to the hospital today and saw it for myself. They hardly let anybody into the intensive care unit. The nurses there seem afraid. We have to be very careful."

"Yes, we do," Isaac said. "I don't know who we can trust. There's one nurse named Vicky. *Maybe* we can trust her. But she's afraid too. I think she's sort of a victim. If we could convince her about what's really going on, she might be on our side."

"We don't have a choice," Grandpa said. "We have to get her on our side. No doctor or police officer will believe us about that mirror box. And the person is very clever and covers their tracks well. We have to be around as much as possible."

"I'll go there early again tomorrow morning," Isaac said. "You can go again during the day. We can hang out there for the whole weekend. We've got to collect as much evidence as we can."

After dinner, Isaac went up to his room and got back on his computer. He felt relieved that there was now an outline of a plan and that Grandpa was well enough to help. He went to Google and typed in "Magic Mirrors."

There were a lot of results, from ancient times to modern, from facts to folktales. He stayed up late reading as much of it as he could.

The earliest information about magic mirrors was reported by Saint Augustine. An area of Greece called Thessaly, a region surrounded by high mountains, was famous in ancient times for the large number of witches living there. The magic in the mirrors belonging to these witches put the witches into a trance. While in this exalted state, they wrote puzzling predictions in an obscure language on the mirrors. The predictions would come to pass—providing they were written in human blood.

Roman generals also had magic mirrors. They used them to look at the results of battles. With the information from the mirrors, they could better plan their battle strategies to conquer their enemies.

In the eleventh century, the bishop of Verona was burned at the stake after a magic mirror was found under his pillow. Written in reverse on the mirror was the word "Fiore," which proved collaboration with the devil, because Satan often appeared in the shape of a flower. A powerful family in the fifteenth and sixteenth centuries, the Medicis had mirrors that they used to find the location of their enemies, so that they could poison them.

Isaac found pictures of fun-house mirrors that warp and distort the viewer. There were mirror mazes, which can look six times as big as they really are because of the reflections. That made them much more confusing than any other kind of maze.

Everyone knows the story of Snow White, in which the vain evil queen has a magic mirror that tells her who the most beautiful in the land is—the mirror is the reason the queen tries to kill Snow White. Isaac learned—he didn't know this until now—that dance studios always have at least one mirrored wall. Dancers watch themselves in the mirror and check that their arms and legs, their heads and shoulders, are in the correct position.

But the mirrors didn't act on their own—they needed a living person to make them work—the same way Joey needed Isaac. The witches of ancient Thessaly used magic mirrors to put themselves into a trance; today, mediums and clairvoyants use the mirrors, Isaac read, to put themselves into a different kind of trance, in which they can communicate with the dead.

Isaac logged off the computer, yawning. Communicating with the dead through a mirror—that's exactly what he had been doing.

22

ISAAC DIDN'T SLEEP WELL THAT NIGHT. Thoughts of what serial killers did to their victims kept running over and over again through his mind.

Of course, being in the hospital, this killer was limited. She—if it was a she—couldn't blatantly *torture* Vera with knives and whips. No, she had to be cunning and subtle. Her form of torture was psychological as well as physical. She could order procedures like endoscopies, which Isaac knew from his own experience were very painful. And who knew what other procedures she was capable of inflicting on people? As with most psychopaths, it was the thrill she got from her victims' suffering that gave her pleasure—because she must be in so much pain herself. And if she actually did kill her patient, she couldn't chop him or her up the way other psychopaths did. Which meant that she had to get her kicks in while Vera was still alive.

Was it a good idea for him and Grandpa to spend as much time at the hospital as possible? Isaac was nervous about provoking Dr. Ciano. But it was the only way to collect more evidence. It was clear that he wasn't welcome at the hospital. He had been forced to undergo that endoscopy and then the MRI without sedation or painkillers of any kind, even though he wasn't a patient. If someone was willing to do that, how far would that person go?

Isaac didn't fall asleep until four A.M. At five thirty, he could hardly bear to get up, but things started early at the hospital. At least it was Saturday and he didn't have to go to school. The weather was getting cooler now, but Grandpa had been thoughtful enough to crank up the heat, so that taking a shower was not frigidly uncomfortable, and it sure helped wake him up. So did the brisk bike ride to the hospital.

Vicky was at the computer when he got to the intensive care unit. She looked exhausted.

"Were you on the night shift?" he asked her.

She nodded unhappily. "And I've got to work the day shift too, without a break. Candi's orders." She dropped her voice. "Candi gives the twins the weekends off. That means more work for the rest of us."

"How's my mother?"

"Actually, she's pretty good . . . mainly because the doctor has been busy for the last couple of days and hasn't been in to see her much—so she hasn't been medicated." Vicky looked around nervously. "I'd better shut up. I shouldn't be telling you this. Go see your mom."

She knew she shouldn't be telling him these things, but she was. That was a hopeful sign. Maybe she was on their side, after all; she also knew that Vera was in trouble. She was tired, which caused her to let her guard down. Isaac made a mental note to remember that.

Isaac peered into Vera's room and saw that his mother was sitting up in bed and eating a little. The bandage on her arm looked smaller now. It was amazing how much she'd improved in such a short time.

She looked up and saw him. "Hi, Ize. Yes, I'm awake, and I feel like eating. The pain in my arm is almost gone. It's great." She dropped her spoon onto the plate. "But they sure know how to ruin oatmeal in this hospital. Just get me out of here, please."

"We won't leave you alone, I promise," Isaac said. Then he sighed. "If only we could get some other doctor to come in, now that they're not drugging you all the time. I bet another doctor would let you out of here. Otherwise, we'll have to escape on our own. I'll be back later today, and Grandpa will be in. He made a steak dinner last night."

Vera shook her head. "Amazing."

Isaac left Vera's room and walked back to the nurses' station.

"When does the doctor come to this floor?" he asked Vicky.

Vicky shrugged. "Hard to say. Usually late in the morning. But don't expect to see her on weekends. She won't be back until Monday."

"Are there any other doctors in the hospital today? Can you page whoever's on call? I think maybe my mother can be discharged." He lowered his voice. "We have to get her away from here, and a good doctor can get her out."

Vicky looked worried. "That's not going to be easy, but let me think about it. Since your mother's a little better, why don't you go on home?"

Vera did seem a little better, so Isaac followed Vicky's suggestion and headed home.

On Sunday, Isaac and Grandpa took turns sitting with Vera. Both agreed that she was looking healthier and acting more alert.

Isaac had been planning to catch up on his homework over the weekend, but he found he still couldn't concentrate. He got out the mirror box Sunday evening and stuck his hands in. Immediately, he felt sleepy.

This time the woman in the mirror was an adult. Her face was clearer now. She was mixing pills again and, as always, muttering to herself in front of the mirror—maybe to distract herself from her own reflection, which she clearly hated.

"It feels good to get back to being productive," she said, smiling almost pleasantly. She was wearing thick turquoise rubber gloves as she worked. Whatever liquid she was working with seemed to be caustic—she didn't dare touch it herself. Was *that* what she had been putting on Vera's arm? Isaac knew he had to get to the hospital before school in the morning.

But he didn't get to sleep until very late and slept through his alarm. Even so, he knew he had to check on Vera and try to catch the attention of another doctor. He was going to have to skip school again. He was doing so poorly in all of his classes now that failure seemed inevitable. But what was more important? He knew what he had to do.

He ate breakfast in five minutes, ran out and jumped on his bike, and was on his way.

23

"I FINALLY GOT TO GO HOME LAST NIGHT," Vicky said to Isaac when he arrived at the hospital. "Man, did I sleep. Came in this morning feeling much better. How are you?"

Isaac was glad she was talking to him like a friend. He hoped he could count on her to help. "Has the doctor come in yet?" he asked her.

"Not yet. How come you're not at school?"

"I'm skipping. Is Candi in?"

"She's with your mother." She nodded at the room. "And the door's closed."

Isaac ran down the hall, then very quietly opened the door and walked inside.

Candi was bending over Vera, who appeared to be unconscious. That's when Issac saw them: the heavy turquoise gloves that he had seen the woman in the mirror wearing. Candi had removed Vera's bandage and was about to apply something to the bruise with wet cotton gauze that she held in a pair of forceps.

"Is that the same acid you were afraid to touch when you were preparing it last night?" Isaac said.

Candi was so startled that she dropped the forceps. The gauze landed on her leg. Even though she was wearing blue scrub pants, the liquid seeped right through the cloth, straight to her leg. She yelped in pain.

"Excuse me," a woman's voice said coldly. Someone squeezed past Isaac into the room. "What's the matter here? What are you doing?"

"That boy! He's always sneaking around. He . . . he . . ."

It was Dr. Ciano. "What could he have done?" she wanted to know. "He's standing in the doorway. You're right next to the bed. Nurse, why is this room so dark? Why is this patient unconscious—again? What's going on?"

Candi was speechless.

The doctor switched on the light.

Isaac could hardly believe it—it *wasn't* Dr. Ciano, after all. It was Candi!

Candi . . . Isaac felt a powerful wave of relief sweep over him. Now he knew who had been hurting Vera, and finally he'd caught her in the act! But he was also worried. Would Dr. Ciano know what was going on and do something to stop it?

"Well?" Dr. Ciano said. "What are you doing with that gauze and those forceps? This patient only had an easily treatable seizure disorder when she came in. She should have been out of here long ago. Patients are waiting for beds. And you keep insisting she can't have another roommate, either. Why is that?"

Isaac's heart lifted.

They both looked at Isaac. Then Dr. Ciano turned back to Candi.

Isaac spoke. "There's acid on that gauze," he dared to say.

"That's a lie! It was just alcohol—see?" Candi held up a bottle. She had somehow managed to switch the bottle of acid with a bottle of plain rubbing alcohol. But she was still on the spot. "Well . . . I mean . . . I'm just concerned about—"

"What *I'm* concerned about is this patient's well-being," Dr. Ciano interrupted. "I've wondered about you before, Ms. Sharpe, even though you've been here for only a short time. What's going on? Why isn't Mrs. Verdi getting any better?"

"Yes, why isn't she?" a male voice said. Grandpa stepped into the room, looking more distinguished than he had in a long, long time.

Candi just stood there, almost crouching, her eyes moving from side to side.

Grandpa walked over to Dr. Ciano and held out his hand. "Bill Costa, Professor Emeritus of Physiology at Washington University Medical School. Vera is my daughter. And we're very worried about her. We don't understand what's happening."

The doctor shook Grandpa's hand, obviously impressed. "Bella Ciano, Neurology. Pleased to meet you. We're puzzled too. Let's take a good look at her. I really don't understand why she's unconscious all the time. And what's happening with her arm? Her diagnosis says osteosarcoma, but there were no symptoms of that when she was admitted. The notes over the weekend indicated that her arm was healing; now its condition is deteriorating again. Her son just said Nurse Sharpe was putting acid on it, but she's denied that. I wish your daughter wasn't unconscious every time I come to see her. It's very strange indeed."

Grandpa didn't say anything; clearly, he knew it would be better to let the doctor figure it out herself—as long as she did before it was too late.

Isaac went over to Vera's bedside with Grandpa and Dr. Ciano. Candi backed away. She must have been worried about what they were going to find— the doctor had seen her with the acid-soaked gauze and the forceps. She could have gone off and tended to another patient, but there was no way she'd leave now. She wanted to be there to try to explain how nothing wrong was happening.

Finally, it was all working out! Dr. Ciano would be able to make things right again. Isaac could hardly believe it.

Then, at the worst possible time, Dr. Ciano's beeper went off.

"Damn!" she muttered to herself. She pulled the beeper out of her pocket. Then she sighed and put it back. "Code 01-05. They need me stat for emergency brain surgery," she explained to Isaac's grandfather. "I'll be back as soon as I can—but sometimes these things go on for hours." She hurried out the door.

No sooner was she gone than Candi stepped forward. She didn't even pretend not to be furious. She was desperate now—the doctor's suspicions had been aroused. "Get out, both of you! You're interfering here!" She said it softly but quickly. Like a cornered rat, she had to act fast. "If you want your mother—and your daughter—to get any better, stay out of it. You're not medical professionals. I am." She focused on Isaac. "Haven't you gotten the message *yet?*"

"I'm not going anywhere," Grandpa replied coolly. "I will call security if I have to. You heard Dr. Ciano's orders. You're not to be anywhere near my daughter." He sat down firmly in the chair next to Vera's bed. "Isaac, I can take care of things here. Go home and catch up on your homework. Come back later."

At the nurses' station Isaac whispered to Vicky, "How long has Candi been here, and where did she come from?"

"Dr. Ciano just asked me the same question as she was leaving—I get the feeling she thinks there's something strange about her. Candi was hired to be in charge of this unit at the end of the summer," Vicky said in a low voice, as though she were telling him something she didn't want anybody else to hear. "She came from County Hospital."

Bingo! Isaac thought.

He rushed home and immediately took out the mirror box and put in his hands. At this point he knew what would happen. He felt sleepy, and waited for the phantom limb to show him another scene.

He was looking out of a different mirror this time. Not into a bathroom but into a hospital room. This room was entirely unlike Vera's; it had a different configuration of furniture and a different type of window. There was a mirror over the sink. The face was no longer blurred. It was Candi, looking just the way she did now. She was washing her hands and saying something, but not to herself. She seemed to be addressing a dim figure in the bed behind her. The room was so dark that Isaac could barely see that there was someone there.

"Amputation is not as bad as people think," Candi said, smiling to herself. The figure in the bed didn't seem to be able to see the smile. Candi dried her hands on a paper towel and tossed it into the trash. Her smile faded as she turned toward the bed. "I mean, God gave us two of so many of our organs— two kidneys, two ears, two eyes. If we lose one of them, the other one takes over. That's why He did it that way. So when you lose an arm or a leg, the other one takes over too. It's as simple as that."

The cracking voice of an adolescent boy came weakly from the bed. "But . . . what about playing the piano? How . . . how can you play the piano without two hands? What if it's . . . the most important thing in your life?"

Candi shook her head, sighed, and clicked her tongue. "Do you always have to be so negative?" she asked the boy. "There's piano music written for the left hand only. I'll find you some. Because I care."

"But . . . that's not really the same. Do my grandparents know? Did the doctor talk to them about it?"

"Don't worry, Joey. Everything will all work out," Candi assured him. "Doctors are very busy. That's why I'm here. It's *my* job to concentrate on the patients who are the most important to me. Like you, my dear." She walked over to the bed, her voice rich with pleasure and warmth. "Your remaining arm will learn to do many things. I've seen other people learn to live with one arm. You'll do better than they did. I know it. Did you know that it takes nineteen muscles to move your hand and wrist? And here's something that will make you feel more comfortable and stop you from worrying all the time." She picked up a large syringe from a tray.

Isaac shook his head and came out of the dream. His hands were still in the mirror box. Now he was even more worried about Candi.

Especially when the phantom limb ripped up another smiley face, more fiercely than the first time.

24

I SAAC RETURNED TO THE HOSPITAL LATE that afternoon. He had to force himself to walk down the hallway past the elevators to the door to the intensive care unit, step by step. He was afraid of what might happen next, and he told himself to stay alert, to keep looking behind him all the time so he wouldn't have to endure more torture.

The twins were again sitting at the door, checking IDs—the easiest job in the hospital. Destiny checked Isaac's without acknowledging him. DCynthia sighed.

When Isaac got to his mother's room, Grandpa told him that he wanted to find Dr. Ciano. He couldn't ask Candi, of course, wherever she was.

While Grandpa was gone, Isaac sat with Vera, who was sleeping.

Vicky came in to check Vera's IV. She was coming in more frequently now to check on her. Isaac asked if Candi had left. She nodded, opened her mouth to say something, then stopped herself. Isaac wanted to ask her what she was going to say, but he didn't want to be pushy.

Grandpa came back soon. "Dr. Ciano's still in emergency surgery. And they wouldn't give me her beeper number. They told me the only person I could talk to was an intern. But . . ." He looked confused for a moment. "But the interns are no help—they're all exhausted and falling asleep. They're too tired most of the time to notice what anybody is doing. We'll just have to wait for Dr. Ciano to come back."

Isaac had an idea. "I'm going to talk to those twins from my school that I told you about," he said. "They're the candy stripers checking IDs."

"I'll stay here. I don't want to leave Vera alone," Grandpa said.

That was fine with Isaac. He wasn't sure how the conversation with the twins would go, but he wanted to do it on his own.

The twins were still sitting at their table. They looked bored.

"Hi," Isaac said.

They looked at him without interest. Then Destiny said, "Here visiting your mommy, twig? Is your grandfather going to stay in the other bed?"

Destiny was so vicious and heartless that it seemed impossible that he could ever get her on his side. But he had to try, because of what he had in mind now—and because he had been successful in getting DCynthia to help him once.

"Candi left for the day, I hear," Isaac said.

Destiny shrugged. "So what?"

He had been hoping they'd volunteer something useful about Candi, but they weren't taking the bait. He'd have to steer the conversation in that direction himself.

"You know, Candi says she's interested in your father. She was really impressed one day when he came to pick you up and she saw his expensive car," Isaac said, making it up.

"That's ridiculous," DCynthia said. "Our father could never like *her*. He already has a girlfriend who's young and hot. We used to hate her, but compared to Candi, she's cool. If Dad ever dated Candi, we'd make their lives a living hell."

It wasn't much, but at least they were starting to open up. Isaac still wasn't sure he could trust them. He decided not to tell them what Candi was doing to Vera right away but instead start at the beginning. "I used to know a kid named Joey," he said. "He went to my old school." That wasn't true either.

"So what?" Destiny said.

"So, he went to another hospital for some little procedure, and Candi was working there—under a different name. She seems to move around a lot. She took care of Joey. He was an amazing piano player—a prodigy, really."

"What's a 'prodigy'?" DCynthia asked him.

"It's one of those show-off words he's always using," Destiny said.

Isaac ignored her. "It's a kid who can play so well that he could give concerts and stuff. But anyway . . . Candi made sure he had his arm cut off."

"Gross!" Destiny said. But she was intrigued. "Tell us more."

"Joey lived with his grandparents, and they were too old or sick or whatever to even come to the hospital, so the doctor and Candi were in control. They said he had bone cancer, but I don't believe it. So they cut off his arm. But he got an infection in the hospital and died."

"What happened next?" DCynthia asked.

"Well, Joey's grandparents put all of their trust in the person taking care of him—Candi. She has this strange power over people," Isaac continued. "Joey's grandparents let her be in charge of his whole treatment."

"So why are you telling us this? What do we care about that kid?" Destiny asked him.

Isaac figured he had already told them this much, he might as well continue. Everybody on the unit already knew about Candi—even Dr. Ciano was beginning to get suspicious. And the more people who knew, the more likely it was that someone would find out everything in time to stop her.

"Because she's trying to do the same thing to my mother. All she had was a seizure disorder when she came in here. Now she has a bad bruise on her arm that wasn't there when she was admitted. And it's getting bigger. The computer says that she has bone cancer, just like Joey. I caught Candi putting something on the bruise today that was so caustic, she wouldn't even touch it herself—she had to wear rubber gloves. Dr. Ciano is finally getting suspicious too. But then she got called away for emergency brain surgery and hasn't come back. My grandfather and I have to get my mother out of here before Candi kills her. We've got to find a way to escape. And I could really use your help. Please." He was only saying this because he was desperate.

Destiny wasn't buying it, of course. "How do you know that's what Candi's doing? Maybe there *is* something wrong with your mother's arm, and she's just trying to help. If Candi really did stuff like that, the hospital would find out and she'd get in big trouble. You're just paranoid because you're a wimp. Count me out."

She was being worse than usual, probably because she was bored and resentful about being at the hospital, where she was forced to help people. She needed to amuse herself by taunting him.

Isaac shrugged. "Fine. Believe whatever you want. But my grandfather *and* Dr. Ciano agree with me about Candi. Even Vicky sees that there's something wrong with her. And *you* know Candi's weird."

"You expect us to feel sorry for you?" Destiny said.

It was hopeless. "Sorry to bother you," Isaac replied, and he turned to leave.

"Wait!" DCynthia said. Destiny shot her a threatening look.

Great. What now? he wondered to himself. They probably just wanted to torment him more, for their own entertainment.

"Why did you say you could really use our help?" DCynthia asked. "Why can't your mother just check out voluntarily?"

"Candi has made it impossible—she told the staff that she's too fragile to be moved. My mother's been unconscious or asleep for most of the time she's been here."

"What about her doctor? Doesn't she have more power than Candi?"

Isaac shrugged. "She did check on my mother, and she became very suspicious of Candi. But then she got called away for emergency brain surgery. Candi's still in charge here, somehow."

"It's a *Candi* unit," Destiny said, laughing. But DCynthia didn't laugh.

"What were you saying about saving your mother?" DCynthia asked him.

"Well, if the doctor doesn't come back soon and do something to stop Candi, I'm going to have to help my mother escape, and fast. I don't think there's much time, the way Candi's treating her." He didn't try to hide the tension in his voice. "We're going to have to get her out of here in some way that nobody will expect, and some way that's fast too, so nobody will have a chance to stop us. They all know that stopping us is what Candi would want them to do."

"I'm going to the café," Destiny announced suddenly and stomped away.

"What do you want us to do?" DCynthia asked Isaac when they were alone.

He shrugged. "I need all the help I can get, and people are used to seeing you around here. The problem is, we have to do it when Candi's not here. And preferably in the middle of the night, when there are fewer people around. There needs to be a diversion that will occupy the staff. I think the two of you would be good at doing that."

"I know I shouldn't—I could get into major trouble with the hospital and my sister—but I'll help you," DCynthia said.

Isaac squeezed her shoulder. "Thanks," he said softly.

Then he noticed that people were wheeling trays of food into the rooms: dinnertime. He was hoping that Vera had woken up and might be able to eat something. "I'll be back in a minute," he said, and he hurried back to her room.

Vera was awake and her dinner had already arrived.

"You'll have to try to eat something. It'll make you stronger, and help you fight those sleeping drugs she's been giving you," Grandpa said.

Vera sat up a little as Grandpa uncovered the largest plate. "Macaroni and cheese," he said. "Not much they can do to ruin that."

"Oh, hi, Ize," Vera said sleepily.

"Maybe you can help her eat," Grandpa said. "I'll get some sandwiches for us down in the café in the main lobby. I'll get Vera some coffee too while we've got the chance. See if you can get her to eat as much as possible." He left the room.

Eating would make her stronger, giving her a better chance to escape.

"If we're going to get out, you've got to eat and get your strength back." Isaac sat down in the chair beside the bed. "That stuff doesn't look so bad. Can you eat it yourself? Or do you need help?"

"I've . . . got to try to do it myself," she said. She picked up a fork shakily and managed to get some macaroni and cheese into her mouth. She chewed slowly, then swallowed with difficulty. "Could be worse."

"You want some ice water?"

"That would help."

Isaac filled a glass with ice at the nurses' station and poured water into it from a bottle in Vera's room. Vera made some headway on the macaroni and cheese and uncovered a dish of salad. "Iceberg lettuce, of course," she said disdainfully, her voice sounding a little stronger.

"After you eat, I want you to try to sit up more," Isaac said. "Then Grandpa and I will help you to stand. It will be easier to get you into a chair and out of here." He was hesitant to tell her about Dr. Ciano's suspicions and scare her more.

His mother lifted her hands, with the IV tubes still inserted. "How can I get out of here when I'm attached to these?" she asked him.

"The pole has wheels on it, but we can easily transfer the bags to the hooks on the chair."

Then Isaac realized the basic flaw in his plan to

help her escape. He knew that none of the nurses, not even Vicky, would remove her IVs. Could he and Grandpa do it themselves?

"Well, if we can get those needles out of you, I have a plan," Isaac said. "And one of those twins from school will help us."

"Twins?" she said, still confused.

Isaac tried to control his impatience. "They're candy stripers on this unit. They know their way around. People are used to seeing them here. We need all the help we can get."

"Why would they help us? Can you really trust them?" Vera said. "The hospital staff would notice right away."

"I can trust one of them. We've got to try *something*!" he said.

Vera had managed to finish a lot of her food by the time Grandpa came back; she must have slept through lunch.

Isaac came up with another idea. "Listen, I've got to go home and get some stuff," he said. "I'll be right back. And then I'll take over, Grandpa, and you can go home and get some rest."

Grandpa nodded. He probably *was* tired, having been there all day, sitting in an uncomfortable chair.

On his way out Isaac stopped at the twins' table. DCynthia was still sitting alone.

"I have to go for a while," Isaac said.

She winked and said, "We'll help your mother escape. I'll tell Destiny that if we work a double shift, we can have tomorrow off. We'll stay here until the middle of the night."

Isaac left and went home. Now that he had a plan, there were still two essential things he needed to make it all work.

The spiral aftereffect and the mirror box.

25

ISAAC WRAPPED THE MIRROR BOX CAREFULLY in a towel and tied it to his bike basket with heavy twine. He also secured the spiral aftereffect to the basket. Then he rode as quickly and carefully as he could back to the hospital.

For a change, Destiny didn't check his ID. "What's all that stuff you got?" she wanted to know.

"Just some things my mother wanted," he said, looking at DCynthia.

The mirror box was cumbersome, and he didn't want to break it during the escape attempt. But he needed Joey's help with something this risky. And the only way to reach him was through the mirror box. He felt safer having Joey along for the ride.

"What's *that?*" Vera asked him as he walked into her room.

"It's the mirror box. If I'm going to be here for a long time, I want the mirror box with me," he said. "I also brought the spiral aftereffect. It worked at school."

Vera looked at Isaac as if he were crazy. "Use that illusion for *what?*" she asked.

Isaac wanted to avoid the question. Luckily, Grandpa interrupted their conversation. "I'm really tired," he said. "I need to go home and get some rest."

"I think you should do that," Isaac said. "I can take care of things here."

After saying good-bye to both of them, Grandpa left.

If the IV needles were going to come out tonight, Isaac would have to do it himself. And Joey could help him—could show him how to safely remove them. He had a lot more experience with hospitals than Isaac or Vera did. And Joey would do anything to get back at Candi.

Vera was wide awake now. There was still no indication of Candi being anywhere nearby. But there was no telling with someone like Candi. She could come back at any time.

Isaac put the mirror box, still wrapped in the towel, on a counter under the window. He washed his hands, then sat down in the chair next to the bed. He wanted to think of something to talk about with Vera, but at the moment he was too preoccupied. He needed to find out how to remove the IV needles. If Joey couldn't tell him, he'd have to somehow trick the information out of Vicky. He also needed to find an escape route. But at the same time, it wasn't safe to leave Vera alone, in case Candi came back. And now that she was alert, she was focused on him. He couldn't do either of the things that he needed to do.

It was barely seven P.M. and Isaac knew they would have to wait until midnight to try to make the break. Vera had been sleeping so much that maybe she'd be able to stay awake on her own, especially with more coffee—just as long as Candi didn't knock her out again. Was it safe to leave her alone long enough to get some more coffee? Now he wished he'd asked Grandpa to stay a few minutes more.

And then, to his immense surprise, Kravetz appeared in the doorway. "How's everything going?" he asked.

"Hey, what are you doing here?" Isaac said. "It's good to see you."

Kravetz nodded at Vera. "Hi. You must be Isaac's mother. I'm Matt Kravetz. I'm in Isaac's class at school. How are you doing?"

"I'm feeling better now, thank you," Vera said, with a genuine smile. "How thoughtful of you to take the trouble to visit."

Isaac knew that Vera was happy that Kravetz had come. But he also knew she was probably even happier that he had made a new friend.

Kravetz shrugged, oddly shy in Vera's presence. "Well, I also know the Fitzpatrick twins, who work here."

He and Isaac exchanged a look. They didn't have to say anything; they both understood. Kravetz wanted to stay in the twins' good graces so Destiny wouldn't turn her venom against him, the way she did against Isaac.

But even so, it would be very convenient to have Kravetz here, if only for a short time.

"Come in. Sit down," Isaac said. "Oh, you're supposed to wash your hands every time you go into a patient's room."

"Yeah, they told me," Kravetz said. He walked over

to the sink, turned on the tap, and pressed down on the liquid soap dispenser. "Is that nurse you were talking about around? I'm curious about her."

"She's not here right now—for a change. It's a relief." He was about to say that was why his mother wasn't doped up and unconscious, but he stopped himself; that might be something Vera wouldn't want him to tell other people. He was dying to tell Kravetz about wanting to escape; Matt might even be able to help. But, again, Isaac didn't think Vera would want him to say anything. Isaac wanted to talk to Kravetz alone. But was it safe to leave Vera?

Then he realized the answer. He couldn't believe he hadn't thought of it before.

"Mom, I'm going to get us some more coffee. We'll need it for tonight. I'll tell that nice nurse, Vicky, to warn you if Candi comes back, and, if she does, to call me right away. We'll only be down in the café for a few minutes." He left her phone next to her.

"I will, Ize, believe me."

"Come on," he said to Kravetz. "We need to be quick."

He stopped by the nurses' station and asked Vicky to warn Vera if Candi came back and gave her his cell phone number. She was happy to oblige, especially now that Vera was alert again. "I just wish Dr. Ciano would get back soon," she said.

"You can say that again," Isaac said.

Kravetz flirted briefly with the twins on his way out of the intensive care unit—he had probably flirted with them on his way in too. That's how he had gotten in there without being related to any of the patients. Destiny beamed and cooed at him.

"You know, Isaac, your mom is kind of a babe," Kravetz said when they got to the elevators.

"Gross!" Isaac said. "That's my mom. But I still can't believe you came to see her."

"It's because of what you said about that nurse," Kravetz said in a low voice. "It sounded like you could use some help." He lowered his voice even more. "Destiny told me you even asked *them* to help you."

"*Destiny* told you that? Well, she doesn't know it, but DCynthia *is* going to help me. It has to be a total surprise. If Destiny tells anyone, it will ruin the whole plan."

"They're famous for their big mouths," Kravetz warned.

"No, we can trust DCynthia. She isn't vicious like Destiny. Destiny's been forcing her to play along."

"I hope you're right about that." Kravetz looked

around. "You need all the help you can get. DCynthia seems to like the idea. She thinks it's exciting, but she doesn't want Destiny to know how she really feels—I could tell. They whispered when they told me about it; they didn't bleat like they usually do."

Isaac couldn't help smiling at the word *bleat*. That was exactly how the twins usually talked, loudly moaning and whining. For a football player, Kravetz had a good vocabulary. But then, Isaac had never known any football players before. Maybe he had the wrong idea about them.

Isaac hesitated when the doors opened and Kravetz entered the elevator. Too embarrassed to let Kravetz know how frightened he was of elevators, he reluctantly stepped in. Somehow, with Kravetz there, the elevator wasn't as bad as it had been that first night when he had taken it without thinking.

The elevator was less crowded at this hour than it was during the day, but Isaac still closed his eyes and took a deep breath. He didn't talk all the way down because it felt as if the other people were too close. He couldn't risk saying anything about their escape plan.

The café was noisier. Isaac checked his watch. They would stay for only five minutes. "That nurse really is a pathological killer," Isaac told Kravetz. "She killed the boy who had the mirror box, and other patients too." He told him about the endoscopy and the MRI he was sure she had ordered for him. "She did it to scare me away. But it didn't work."

"Do you think the twins might be in danger too?" Kravetz asked.

"I think they're safe from her. She only seems to target piano players—like the boy who had the mirror box, and my mother."

"How do you know all this stuff about that nurse, anyway?"

Isaac felt he could trust Kratevz, so he told him about the phantom limb and what it showed him. He explained the Macdonald Triad. "You can try out the mirror box—it's up in my mother's room. But the phantom limb probably won't appear for you. It's shy. It wouldn't show itself to my grandfather."

Kravetz shook his head. "I'd think you were crazy, except . . . for some reason I don't."

Isaac told him exactly what Candi was doing to Vera—the diagnosis of bone cancer he had seen on the hospital computer, and the fact that her doctor hadn't been the one to make that diagnosis. He told him that he faced two challenges: finding a route out of the hospital without being noticed and getting the IVs out of Vera's hands without hurting her.

"But what makes it so hard is that I can't leave my mother alone. My grandfather's already been with her all day, and he's old. *I* have to guard her."

"I know all about giving shots and removing needles," Kravetz said. "I learned it in this advanced first aid course my parents made me take at the junior college when I went out for football."

"You're kidding!" Isaac said.

"I'm not kidding. And I have time to look around the hospital, see if there's a map or something. You go back up to the room and watch your mother. I'll be back as soon as I find a route."

Isaac couldn't believe how eager Kravetz was to help. If this was Matt's way of saying he was his friend, then Isaac was more than happy to accept.

Back in the intensive care unit, Vicky told him Candi still hadn't come back. "She already worked the morning shift. No normal person would be back until tomorrow morning. But with her, you never know."

Vera was still alert and reading to pass the time. She put her book down when Isaac came in with her coffee.

"Oh," he said. "Did Grandpa tell you that Dr. Ciano was here?"

She sighed. "Yes. He said she was suspicious of Candi, but then had to leave because of emergency surgery. If only she'd come back."

"When I first got here, before Grandpa did, I caught Candi putting something caustic on your bruise, right before the doctor came. She stopped when she saw me, but she dropped it on her leg and it burned her through her pants."

"But . . ." Vera seemed close to tears. "Why is she hurting me so much, on purpose?" Vera protected her bruised arm by putting it under the sheet. "How could such a maniac be working as a nurse?"

"It's complicated, Mom," Isaac said. "If Dr. Ciano comes back, that would solve everything. But if she doesn't come back in time, Matt's going to help us with your escape. Tonight."

"But what about this thing I'm attached to?"

"Matt knows all about how to administer needles. He took an advanced first aid course at the junior college. And he's off looking for an escape route now."

Her eyes widened. "You're kidding. You really think you can get me out of here?"

"We have to. When Matt comes back, he can work on the needles."

"He seems like a really nice guy. I didn't know you had made such a nice friend. Why didn't you tell me?"

"It just happened. And you were asleep all the time. Plus I didn't think he was really my friend until he showed up here just now."

Yes, the whole idea of escaping was scary. But it was exciting too. It would be wonderful to beat Candi.

While Matt was gone, Isaac figured he had enough time to find out if the phantom limb had anything new to tell him. Vera was still sipping her coffee. The counter under the small window was just big enough for the mirror box.

"Do you mind if I take a minute to look at this?" Isaac said. "I might learn something that could help us." He carefully began unwrapping the mirror box.

Vera rolled her eyes. "Go ahead. But I don't see how that thing can help you."

"That's just it—it may be the *only* thing that can help us. It shows me things, like Candi as a teenager preparing to set fire to the cabin at camp."

Vera raised her eyebrows skeptically but remained silent. She watched him attentively.

Isaac unwrapped the mirror box carefully and set it on the towel on the counter. He knelt on the floor in front of it and stuck in his hands. Right away his eyes began to droop.

He was again inside Candi's current bathroom mirror. She was wearing her turquoise rubber gloves and pawing through an oversized turquoise bag. *"Darn!"* she said. (It was interesting that she didn't say *damn.* Maybe she thought cursing was immoral.) "Why is there so much stuff in here? Where did I drop that IV bag, anyway?"

She sighed and chewed on her lip, staring straight into the mirror, thinking out loud. "It wasn't in the elevator, it wasn't in the basement. Could I have dropped it when I came out onto that ramp at the loading dock?"

Loading dock? Ramp? That was accessible via the basement? That would be a great way to get out of the hospital. Unlike the big front door in the lobby, there might not be anybody at the loading ramp in the middle of the night—no staff, no security. That must have been why Candi chose that exit on her way out after stealing the IV bag to put some of her own drugs in it. He had the strong feeling that this scene was taking place right now, at this very minute.

"They're ruining everything for me," Candi said through gritted teeth. "Otherwise, I could have put this special medication in the IV bag right at the hospital. But I won't let them stop me!"

Isaac's strategy had worked! Having someone constantly in the room had interrupted Candi's plan—for now, at least.

Candi wasn't wearing her nurse's scrubs, though. She was wearing a turquoise dress, her favorite color.

26

ISAAC! WHAT'S THE MATTER WITH YOU? ARE you in a trance or what? Your friend's here."

"Huh?" Isaac blinked, then pulled his hands out of the box. But he had just enough time to notice the phantom limb running along on two fingers. It was telling Isaac they had to escape now!

He turned around to see Vera staring at him. Kravetz was standing in the doorway.

"Candi's not here," Isaac said. "She's at home. And there's a loading dock, with at least one ramp, at the back of the hospital. That's the best place to get out. There probably won't be anybody there in the middle of the night; staff and security will be at the main entrance and in the ER."

Kravetz was holding several papers in his hand. "How do you know about all of that? And how did you know about the loading dock? You didn't say anything about it in the café," he said, baffled.

"The mirror box just showed me."

"Jeez! Lemme see that thing," Kravetz said, walking quickly over to the box. He looked it over tentatively, as if he didn't know what to expect.

Sensing his anxiety, Isaac calmly said, "Put both your hands in the holes. Then move your right hand but not your left, and look in the right side of the mirror."

Kravetz followed Isaac's instructions. Vera was watching too. Like everybody else, Kravetz flinched when he first felt the sensation. "Whoa!" he exclaimed. "It feels like I have an invisible third hand . . . like my real left hand is paralyzed or something. This thing is just as weird as that spiral effect thing you had. But . . . how can it tell you and show you things? I wouldn't believe it, except you found out about the loading ramp, and you didn't seem to know about it when we talked in the café."

Isaac told him the whole story—what the box had shown him about Candi and Joey. Vera listened raptly too; this was the first time he had told her everything in so much detail.

Kravetz lowered his voice. "Well, now I can really see why you have to escape."

"I just hope that we can trust DCynthia, and that Destiny won't blow it for us," Isaac said. "I want to believe that DCynthia will help, but I don't know for sure."

Kravetz stood up. "You need more than DCynthia's help. You need Destiny's help too. I'll go and talk to her now, and try to convince her. This is going to take a lot of planning—if we can carry it off at all." He left the room.

Vera looked at Isaac. "Gee, Ize, now I'm almost starting to believe you about the mirror—"

Vicky came in at that moment to check on Vera.

"I need to use the bathroom," Vera said.

"I'll bring a bedpan," Vicky said, smiling.

"No. I want to use the bathroom," Vera said.

Isaac was glad to see Vera wanting to do something on her own.

"OK. I think we can try that. I'll go get an aid," Vicky said.

Isaac left the room and walked quickly around the intensive care unit.

The escape was beginning to seem possible. He hadn't counted on Vera being able to walk more than a few feet, but now maybe she could. He knew she would be weak, though. This was the first time she was trying to stand up since she'd become bedridden.

Then he noticed two orderlies. Carefully, he followed them. They didn't go far, just a short way down the hall to a door with no number on it. They opened the door without unlocking it. It had to be some kind of storage room. Isaac waited until they emerged, then approached them.

"Excuse me," he said to them. "Is there a wheelchair in there?"

"Yes, this is where they're stored," one of them said.

Isaac made his way back to Vera's room, which was open a little. He went in.

Vera was wiping her eyes. "That was so *embarrassing!*" she said faintly. "I couldn't get to the bathroom. I had to use the bedpan with the nurse and the aid. I never want to have to go through that again. I just don't understand what happened to my *legs*." She sounded as if she was going to start crying again.

Had Candi been giving her drugs that did more

than just knock her out? Isaac had never been so angry at anyone in his life. And that increased his determination.

"Candi must have done it. She wasn't just knocking you out, she was progressively making you weaker. Now do you understand why we have to get you out of here *tonight*? Any way we can."

Vera nodded.

"If they try to give you sleeping pills, don't take them," Isaac said. "Hold them in your mouth and then spit them out later. Whatever you do, don't swallow them."

"It's always been Candi, but it's always in the IV, as far as I can tell," Vera said. "If she doesn't come back tonight, maybe nobody will give me anything."

"Well, Vicky knows you've been knocked out all the time. I'll go and tell her to lay off. That might give us a chance to get out of here. Be right back."

He went to the nurses' station and found Vicky. "Excuse me," he said, "but you saw that something's wrong with my mother's legs. She's still not doing well, even though she's more coherent. Remember how the doctor didn't like it that she's unconscious so much?"

"Yes, I do," Vicky said.

"Don't you think it might be better if you stopped giving her any medications while we have the chance?"

Vicky was in total agreement. He didn't have to say, "Until Candi comes back and starts them all over again."

"They're not giving you anything," Isaac told Vera back in the room. "We're safe until Candi returns. And now I've found out where the wheelchairs are. We can use one to help you escape."

"Thank you, Ize. That's a relief. What would I do without you and Grandpa? I've never felt so helpless in my life, and I don't like it. I don't like it at all! Even when your father was around I was independent, and I want to keep it that way. I'll do anything to get away from here. And as soon as I'm out, we'll call the police."

Kravetz came back around eight thirty, smiling. "It's all taken care of. I asked Destiny out. I think DCynthia knew it was an act, and she played along. They told their father they had to stay late tonight. I was right there when they called him. They promised they'd create a diversion to help us. Destiny seemed to be really into it."

Isaac remembered what Kravetz had said: "If *we*

can carry it off." Did that mean he was going to stay, along with the twins, and help with the escape? That would make a huge difference.

"I didn't show you the maps yet," Kravetz said. He took some folded-up sheets of paper from his pocket. "Here's the basement. It's one floor below the lobby level. There are loading docks with ramps on the side and along the back—if you use the side one, it's not too far from the elevators."

"What if it's locked?" Isaac asked him.

"Don't worry—I unlocked it," Kravetz said. "Besides, even a little while ago, there was hardly anybody around. Late at night it ought to be pretty deserted."

"Thanks. This is great," Isaac said. He folded up the map of the basement and put it in the pocket of his jeans.

Although Isaac's main priority was still Vera, he couldn't help but see this whole thing as an adventure, especially now that they had a plan. And best of all, Isaac wasn't doing it alone anymore. He had friends who were going to help him, and that made all the difference in the world.

27

BUT KRAVETZ WASN'T ABLE TO HELP HIM, after all.

His father had called, reminding him that it was a school night and telling him it was too late to be staying at the hospital. Kravetz had argued and pleaded, but there was no way he could convince his father without telling him exactly what was going on. And there was no way his father would've believed him.

It was eleven thirty, and he had to leave. He reluctantly went home.

Before he left, he brought Isaac and Vera more coffee. Then—after they closed the door so that the nurses couldn't see—Kravetz, working extremely carefully, removed the needles from the veins on the backs of Vera's hands. She winced as he did it, and looked scared, but there was almost no blood. He cleaned the cuts with antiseptic from the medicine cabinet next to the sink and bandaged her hands, and then he taped the needles back in place on top of the veins, so it would look as if she was still attached to the IV lines. He also figured out how to turn the machine off so that the fluid was no longer dripping into the lines. All Isaac had to do before he and his mother made their break was to remove the tape and Vera would be free of the IVs.

Isaac had hoped Kravetz would be there to run interference for them, the way he did when he was playing football, just in case the orderlies should come along. Still, he was very grateful to Kravetz for all he had done. Despite everything, it gave him a warm feeling knowing how much Kravetz had risked to help them.

But now Isaac would have to engineer the escape alone with an unstable Vera. Would the spiral aftereffect do its job? It was a good thing the twins were going to make a diversion—he hoped—to capture the attention of the staff on this unit.

The floor was quiet now. The other patients seemed to be asleep. No bells were ringing, and there were no PA announcements. When Isaac looked down the hall, the two nurses at the station appeared to be drowsy. Then one of them got up and left. Now there was only one nurse there.

He looked back at Vera and saw that her eyes had slipped shut. After all that coffee? He was going to have to wake her up. It was quarter to twelve now. Maybe he should let her rest for five minutes. He was feeling pretty sleepy himself. What harm would it do if he shut his eyes too for just five minutes?

No! If he gave in, he would fall asleep. They had to start now. There was no more putting it off. He went and got a wheelchair.

And then he heard a commotion unlike anything that had ever happened on the floor before—two loud bratty voices hurling insults at each other.

"You rotten, two-timing bitch! How could you tell her? He trusted us. And everything he said about her is true and you know it."

"Oh, shut up! You must have a crush on that twig, you sap." A cackle of witchlike laughter followed. "You're falling for that jerk, DCynthia? You're pathetic!"

There was a rattling crack, and then a shriek. "DCynthia! You broke my new phone! I'll kill you for that!"

The twins. Fighting about something. Disturbing every patient on the unit in the middle of the night . . . and attracting the attention of the staff!

It was time to leave.

"Mom. Wake up. We gotta go."

Vera didn't stir.

Isaac shook her shoulder. Her eyes blinked open. "Huh?"

He carefully untaped the needles from the backs of her hands. He let them hang from the lines attached to the plastic bags on the IV poles. She was still blinking, confused, not yet fully awake.

A crashing of glass, the sound of bodies tumbling to the floor. Another cracking thud. "Now you've wrecked *my* phone, Destiny!"

"Loser! You deserved it."

He heard running footsteps—the hospital staff was arriving to break up the fight. The twins' distraction was actually working.

"Mom. Come *on*! We've got to get you into this wheelchair." He gently lifted her up into a sitting position, then pulled down the railing on the side of the bed. He maneuvered her legs, in pink hospital pajama pants, over the side of the bed, and positioned her feet on the floor. She seemed to be waking up, and the more awake she became, the more tense she appeared. Her eyes were furtive, her mouth a hard line.

He pushed the wheelchair as close to the bed as he could get it. He had to hurry. He knew the staff would subdue the twins quickly. "OK, now you've got to stand up so we can get you into this chair. We don't have much time!" He tried to lift her by her elbows, but she was deadweight. She slid back down onto the bed.

Isaac panicked. He couldn't do it by himself.

Just then the door opened and Kravetz walked in.

"Hey, I'm back. I didn't go home. I'll deal with my father later." He saw what Isaac was trying to do and told him to get on the other side of his mother.

With Matt's help, Isaac was easily able to lift Vera into the chair. Vera trusted both of them and went along with what they were doing.

Isaac looked out the door. The nurses' station was deserted. Everybody must be dealing with the twins, whom he could still hear screaming at each other down the hall.

"You moron, DCynthia! I'm going to scratch your face with this broken phone so deep that no plastic surgeon will ever be able to fix it! You'll be a freak for the rest of your life!"

At the last second, Isaac remembered the mirror box. He had to have it with them when they left. He wasn't sure why, he just knew he wanted the phantom limb along, and something seemed wrong about leaving Joey behind. He set the mirror box carefully in Vera's lap. "Hold on tight to this. It's more important than you know," he told her. He took out the spiral aftereffect.

They pushed the wheelchair as fast as they could past the nurses' station and down the hall toward the exit.

Near the doors to the intensive care unit the twins were wrestling on the floor, pulling each other's hair. The night staff was kneeling around them, trying to drag them apart. Isaac had to give both of the twins credit: they had picked a spot that gave the three of them access to the exit.

But just as they reached the doors, the orderly who had taken Isaac down to the MRI looked up and saw them. "Hey!" he shouted. "What the hell do you think you're doing?"

Isaac pushed through the doors. He could hear the sounds of people running after them, voices that were not the twins' calling out, *"Stop! Stop!"* Despite the twins' display, they hadn't avoided being noticed. Their pursuers were close behind.

Matt kept pushing the chair. Isaac knew he wouldn't have been able to do this himself.

He turned around and brandished the spiral aftereffect, holding it at eye level, spinning it all the way to number ten. He aimed it at their pursuers, all the while continuing to hurry backward, staying as close as he could to the wheelchair.

Two male orderlies and three female nurses were following. Behind them were the twins, disheveled and limping. Vicky wasn't there, but the others were coming fast. It took a few moments, but then their eyes were caught by the spiral aftereffect. Would they look at it long enough for it to work?

Isaac took a chance and stopped. If he stood still, they might focus on the spiral aftereffect and slow down.

The spiral aftereffect whizzed around.

Their pursuers did indeed slow down. Their eyes were riveted on the spiral aftereffect. One of the nurses crumpled to her knees, and then the tall orderly tripped as well. Isaac started moving backward again, taking a quick glance around to see where Vera and Matt were. They had reached the elevators. He hurried to join them.

Matt was pressing the up and the down buttons furiously, just wanting to get away. Isaac started to panic. He grabbed the mirror box out of Vera's lap and held it tightly.

He knew he had to concentrate on the people following them. Luckily, those who were still standing were moving much slower now. There was, he figured, a slight chance that he, his mother, and Matt could actually escape . . . if the elevator came in time.

A chime sounded, and an elevator going up arrived. Isaac rushed in, stifling his claustrophobia. There were more important things now. Unexpectedly, the doors quickly slammed shut, closing before Matt and Vera could get on. There had to be somebody else on the elevator for the doors to close so fast. Isaac turned around to see who it was.

Candi.

28

CANDI WAS WEARING THE SAME TURQUOISE dress she had on when the mirror box showed her in her bathroom. She was carrying the large fake leather turquoise bag as well.

She smiled when she saw Isaac. "Looks like your friends aren't so trustworthy," she said. "I knew I could count on Destiny. She called me and told me you were going to try to get your mother out. I rushed here immediately. My strict orders forbade your mother from leaving her room, and that she be kept on her medications. I'm the professional, and I know what she needs in order to get well."

"There's nothing wrong with my mother, and you

know that. You hate her for some weird reason . . . for playing the piano."

"*You!*" she said. She was furious, even though she still spoke in her habitually soft voice. "It's all your doing, you little pest! I never should have allowed you on the floor. Well, I'll take care of that now. You'll never go anywhere again." She reached into her bag and pulled out a long scalpel, so sharp that it glittered in the light. She advanced on Isaac.

Candi was inches away from him when the elevator stopped and the door behind her opened. Dr. Ciano stepped on. She jerked and looked suddenly alert when she saw Candi with the scalpel.

"Nurse Sharpe!" she shouted, grabbing Candi by the arm. "Have you completely lost your mind? I suspected it before, but now I know it. I'm calling security!" With her other hand she reached for the alarm button.

"No!" Candi wailed. "This is my whole life! This is everything I have!"

At that moment, the elevator reached the basement. The door in front of Isaac opened. Candi suddenly twisted away from Dr. Ciano and lunged for him, but he was a step ahead of her. He jumped through the door before it had fully opened and ran as fast as he could, holding the mirror box in front of him, with the spiral aftereffect on top of it.

Candi swung the scalpel wildly at Dr. Ciano, grazing her arm, then took off after Isaac.

Dr. Ciano stood there frozen, paralyzed from shock. The door slammed shut with her still inside the elevator.

The basement. This was the dark hallway where Isaac had been sent for the hellish endoscopy and MRI. And now Candi was chasing after him with a deadly sharp scalpel. She was moving fast.

The map Kravetz had given him, the one that showed where the exit ramps were, was in his back pocket. But he had no time to stop, pull it out, and study it, especially while holding the mirror box and the spiral aftereffect. All he could do was hope to outrun Candi. He pictured the scalpel and knew that she was pointing it directly at his neck.

"You'll never get away from me, you little troublemaker. I know this place like the back of my hand, and you don't know it at all!"

He passed the torture chamber of the endoscopy room. Then the floor ahead of him sloped down, into a darker, smaller hallway, like a tunnel. Another uncomfortably confined space. He had no choice but to follow its path. He kept running until he could barely see.

Thick pipes hung from the ceiling. The floor was uneven, making him stumble. He could hear Candi's heavy breathing getting closer.

In the dimness to his left he could barely make out a metal door. Did he have time to stop and try to open it? He glanced around for a second. Candi was ten feet behind him. As he watched, she dropped the scalpel, reached into her bag, and pulled out an amputation drill saw, just like the one Joey had showed him in the mirror.

Cradling the mirror box and the spiral aftereffect under one arm, Isaac pulled on the metal doorknob and the door opened. He rushed inside and slammed the door shut behind him. There was only a fluorescent light in here, flickering dimly, but it gave enough light for him to see that there was no lock on the door. He had run into a trap.

He looked frantically around in the few seconds he had before Candi entered, hoping there were tools in here that he could use as weapons. No tools. There was only a large machine with two big fat wheels of white gauze on a bar at the bottom, and above them a complex structure that looked like a loom of some kind. He had no idea what it was for, only that it had no use for him to protect himself.

Candi pulled open the door with her left hand and slammed it shut behind her. Brandishing the drill saw in her right hand, she stared at Isaac. He backed up as best he could against the machine, but it was full of sharp edges and angles.

And then she smiled. "You're even stupider than I thought," she said. "If you'd stayed out there in the tunnel, you could have gotten out on one of the loading ramps. But now you're stuck. That gauze folder will pierce you if you get any closer."

She moved toward him.

She was right. He couldn't back up any more. He could feel the machine cutting into his T-shirt. The flickering light was dim, but there was enough for him to see the razorlike ridges of the saw blade coming closer and closer to his neck. Candi pressed a switch. The saw began to turn, its piercing high-pitched scream like the sound of a dentist's drill, only louder.

He kicked out at her, but it had no effect. Her abdomen was hard as a rock. Killing people was clearly better exercise than riding a bike. Candi was a lot stronger than he had expected.

The drill saw lashed out. If Isaac didn't think of something quickly, he was as good as dead. He looked down at his hands.

He set the mirror box on the floor beside him and held up the spiral aftereffect. He set it on ten and it began spinning.

Candi's eyes couldn't avoid it. They fixed on it immediately. She'd never seen anything like it before. She stopped moving toward him.

"I know what you've done, Candi," Isaac said, gaining confidence because he had slowed her down.

Candi lowered the drill saw, completely transfixed by the spiral aftereffect.

"I know you killed Joey Haynes," Isaac went on. "Because he played the piano. And I know you've killed other people before him. People who also played the piano. And now you want to kill my mother. What do you have against piano players, Candi?"

She opened her mouth, then closed it. "I . . . I . . ." Her eyes were staring at the spiral aftereffect. Now Isaac had her trapped.

"You even killed your own brother!" he shouted at her.

"Don't talk about my brother!" she screamed, her voice suddenly returning to her. She viciously moved toward him again, the drill saw now raised above her head.

Isaac quickly lowered the spiral aftereffect so that it was out of her field of vision.

Candi stumbled and fell to her knees. She seemed completely disoriented. "You've gotten in my way ever since you first showed up," she said, sounding as if she was going to cry. She struggled to her feet. "And now I'm going to stop you for good."

"You'll never get away with it. Dr. Ciano knows now. And security will be here any second."

"I'll get away with it, all right. I know how to get out of here from the loading docks," she said fiercely, her fury returning. "I'll disappear. They'll never find me. I've done it before, and I can do it again." She swiped at Isaac with the drill saw and knocked the spiral aftereffect out of his hands.

He was helpless. He had no weapon to use against her. All he had was the mirror box. He had put it on the floor, and now he was shielding it from Candi, standing between it and her.

And then, without warning, incredibly—there was no other way to describe it—Isaac and Candi were *sucked into* the mirror box. It was just like the times it had sucked in the stick of licorice and then the piece of paper with Isaac's questions on it. Isaac felt a rushing, pulling sensation. The box grew larger and larger. It was as though he was being dragged underwater by a powerful undertow.

And then they were *inside* the box.

But it didn't look like the inside of the box. He was standing in front of a gigantic cube, as high as a six-story building. It was full of square holes. He knew exactly where he was.

It was the Menger sponge—the strange object he had in his collection in which every chamber was horribly smaller than the one before. There was nothing else to be seen—he was on an endless plane with the sponge.

He heard footsteps behind him and turned around. Candi was running toward him, still pointing the drill saw at him. She was getting closer.

There was no place to go but into the Menger sponge. It was so big that the largest hole was high above him. He began to climb, using smaller holes to grip with his hands and put his feet in. It was amazing how fast he got to the top, and then he was inside.

He was in a vast hall with black empty windows all around. He heard Candi climbing behind him. He headed for the biggest hole. It was hard to move quickly because the floor was pitted with holes. He reached the hole, climbed halfway up the wall, and got inside. Now he was in a space the size of a movie theater. He could still hear Candi behind him, so he frantically kept climbing. The next hole was the size of a living room. He began to sweat. He turned and looked behind him. Candi was just entering the room with her drill saw still turning.

He ran for the next room. This cubic space was the size of a bathroom. He could almost *feel* the walls closing in around him. A horrible sinking feeling set in, and he knew that he was really trapped now. He was like somebody in a horror movie, running from the monster by going up into the attic. Any room he went into would be smaller than the one he was in. But where else could he go?

Nowhere . . . except into the next room, which was the size of a closet. He could hear Candi breathing heavily right behind him. And on into the next room, which was so small he couldn't stand up. Then into the next, which was so tiny that he had to crouch down into a ball. He was panting, and his clothes were soaked with sweat.

And then he was shrinking, becoming so tiny that the space became the size of the first vast hall he had entered. He climbed to the next biggest hole, but now he knew it was hopeless. Because what had happened before was happening again, repeating itself on a miniature level. Every space he entered got smaller and smaller. It was infinite. He was never going to get away from Candi. It was a cycle he'd never break. Never, never, never . . .

"Good-bye, my friend," a voice said. "And thank you for bringing her to me. I couldn't do it on my own."

Isaac was standing in the hospital basement again, next to the gauze folder, with the mirror box at his feet. It was the first time he had heard Joey's voice.

Joey had saved him.

But Candi wasn't there. She must still be in the mirror box, thought Isaac. Joey had gotten her because of what Isaac had done with the spiral aftereffect.

"Hello, Candi," Joey said.

29

One month later.

REALLY, THERE'S NOTHING ELSE TO SAY. My friends found me in the basement. Miss Sharpe felt cornered, and she ran. She's out there somewhere," Isaac said politely to the reporter and hung up the phone.

"My grandson, the celebrity." Grandpa chuckled.

"Hey, Ize, are you still giving autographs?" Kravetz asked.

Their laughter was interrupted by a knock at the door. A UPS man was holding two large boxes, one marked FRAGILE. He was standing at the open doorway of the new house that Vera, Grandpa, and Isaac had moved into a few weeks earlier.

"My collection! I thought they were lost forever," Isaac said as he ran to the door. "Careful, they're fragile. Hey, Matt, wait until you see these."

"Thank you," Grandpa said. He smiled as he watched Isaac and Matt carefully climb the stairs, each holding a box.

Upstairs, the two boys gently placed the boxes on a table in the attic of the small, sunny house. Like a skilled surgeon, Isaac cut open the boxes and removed the carefully wrapped contents. The process was long and tedious, but necessary.

When everything was unpacked, Isaac knew something was missing. It was the mirror box. Instinctively, he understood why it wasn't there. Isaac had given it what it wanted, and it had given Isaac what he needed.

"Hey, man, what's this?" Matt asked, getting Isaac's attention.

"It's the Menger sponge," Isaac said. "I'll tell you about it sometime."

Downstairs, Vera's next student arrived for her piano lesson.

About the Authors

WILLIAM SLEATOR met ANN MONTICONE while they both worked at the Boston Ballet. He was the pianist and she made costumes. Their friendship was cemented when they discovered that their favorite movie is *Bride of Frankenstein*. They have previously collaborated on the book *Test* together. Ann lives in Boston and teaches at an elementary school. William divides his time between homes in Boston and Thailand.

This book was designed by Maria T. Middleton. The text is set in 11-point ITC New Baskerville, a revival typeface reinterpreted by John Quaranda in 1978 and based on the original eighteenth-century classic created by John Baskerville. The display font is Webster Roman.

This book was printed and bound by R.R. Donnelley in Crawfordsville, Indiana. Its production was overseen by Erin Vandeveer.